# CAROL DRINKWATER

**■SCHOLASTIC**

For Walter, Florence and Clara; Peter and Dennis...
Always in my heart.

Scholastic Children's Books
Euston House, 24 Eversholt Street,
London, NW1 1DB, UK

A division of Scholastic Ltd
London ~ New York ~ Toronto ~ Sydney ~ Auckland
Mexico City ~ New Delhi ~ Hong Kong

Published in the UK by Scholastic Ltd, 2014

Text copyright © Carol Drinkwater, 2014
Cover photography © Jeff Cottenden, 2014

ISBN 978 1407 13895 4

Printed and bound in the UK by CPI Group UK (Ltd), CR0 4YY

2 4 6 8 10 9 7 5 3 1

The right of Carol Drinkwater and Jeff Cottenden to be identified as
the author and cover photographer of this work has been asserted by
them in accordance with the Copyright, Designs and Patents Act, 1988.

# JUNE 1916
## DENNIS

Day was breaking on what was to be a hot one. My mother, bone-thin, leaning close to the creaking green gate out on the cracked paving stones, was waving me goodbye with her handkerchief. This is my last mental picture of home. Her face was immobile but I knew she hated the prospect of our separation and the dangerous uncertainty about my future. My return. England has been at war with Imperial Germany for almost two years and the losses have been far greater than ever anticipated. Still, I think my mother had convinced herself that I was out of harm's reach. I could have volunteered as a private in the infantry soon after war was declared, but I had an accident in my dad's workshop and broke three toes on my left foot. The army didn't want to take me for as long as I hobbled. The foot took its time healing and I was obliged to stay home. But last month conscription was introduced and my toes were right as rain, so I had to go. Off to war.

\*

I waved one more time. My mother, Florrie Stoneham, watched me silently until I rounded the corner with my kitbag on my back. Troubles packed, as they say.

I was on my way. At last.

*

I am twenty years old. A few months off being a man, yet I know I am still as soft as a crinkle-haired boy in many ways. My name is Dennis, and until these past few weeks I have lived with my mum and dad in Islington, London. My dad, Walter Stoneham, "Wallie" to my mum, is a master carpenter and cabinet-maker and he is training me to be as skilled in the craft of joinery as he is. It's a good living and there is plenty of work to be had for those who are serious about it. The problem is, my heart is not in it. Music, the entertainment business, is where my passions lie. If I could, I would like to play and write songs all day long. I had been hoping that distancing myself from Dad's workshop would give me ample opportunity to concentrate on my music, but all that I am carrying in my kitbag is a penny whistle. Without my musical instruments – my piano, banjo and ukulele – I will find it hard to write songs and will feel like a poor young man.

*

I was given orders to join my battalion and board a train at Waterloo station, close by the River Thames. I was looking for the South Western Railway line to Southampton, but I couldn't miss it; there must have been a thousand blokes in uniform, slouching against their kitbags or sitting on the platform leaning against their belongings, smoking, chatting, dreaming or worrying, waiting to embark. Many of them, like me, lowly rankers and nervous new conscripts.

*

Southern England in the early summer is a fine sight even though the country is at war. There were plenty of allotments crammed up against one another, bursting with maturing vegetables. Rickety fences demarcated one patch from the other. I was travelling with loads of other lads. My regiment was a raucous bunch. We were all crushed up together; scared and excited strangers on our way out into the world to fight for our King and country. For many of the others, though, this was not their first outing to the Front. They knew the ropes, one boasted to me, and I would have to wait to see it for myself. We were edging west to the port of Southampton. From there a ship was awaiting us, to sail us to Le Havre. I had never been on a ship before, except once as a kid on the River Thames outside London, but that was a rowing boat, a far more humble means of transport.

We hadn't been given the details of our final destination, although we knew it was in France, to somewhere they were calling the Western Front. France is a big country and I have no geography. I couldn't have said if it were to the right or left of London, but it stood across from a strip of water south of London known as The Channel. A channel of water. The French call it "the sleeve".

*

We reached the coast by midday. The lower fringes of England. This southern shore faces towards the continent, but you could not see across to the other side because it lies some twenty nautical miles away, or so one of the other conscripts told me. This was not my first sighting of the sea, although it was for some of the lads. I had been taken once on a family outing to Brighton, but I had been too young (and stroppy!) to recall most of the details. My parents had been heading off to the races with my aunt Clara and her husband, Bertie. They own a florist shop in Holborn, another part of London and quite close to Islington. My aunt loves a "flutter on the gee-gees". All dressed up in their finery they were, furs and bags and glittering buttons, intending to make a weekend of it at the Brighton Races. The horse and buggy was outside waiting to take them to the railway station at London Bridge, but I bawled so loudly when they tried to leave me that they were obliged to take me along with them, and so I got to spend a day down on the South Coast. Spoiled, I was.

*

The stretch of sea I was looking at in Southampton was different. It was a bustling, stinking, oil-slicked port, awash with liners and steamers; jam-packed with any seaworthy carrier the military could lay its hands on. All were being made ready for the transportation of young men, like myself, across the brine to war. The intense busyness and inevitability of it all quite made my stomach churn.

I felt less troubled, more at home, when, amidst the mayhem, I caught sight of a crew of stevedores unloading a shipment of hardwood timber from an impressive civilian vessel that had sailed all the way from India, one of the porters told me. I stood gazing in wonder. There must have been a felled forest aboard that craft. *Dad could make fine use of all that*, I thought, pining quietly for home and for the workshop and comfortable life I was saying farewell to.

After a spot of lunch, before embarkation, three of the other blokes in my regiment – Charley Woods, Ginger Green and Bobby Masters – Masters is a regular and our corporal; sharp-nosed, a little sharp of tongue too, but he seems a decent sort – took me into Southampton town to stock up on some useful accessories: soap, boot brushes, lots of notepaper and pencils, a small packet of handkerchiefs, a penknife, a stamp and a comb. All tucked away neatly into my kitbag.

Our ship was due to sail at ten p.m., so after the shopping we had the remainder of the afternoon and early evening to kill, kicking our heels about the town. Our last breath of England this port was to be. For a while or forever? How many of us would make it back? I felt a bit queasy at this thought and determined not to dwell on it.

Most of the other blokes slid off for a couple of pints. Ginger Green, all of six-foot-three and clearly a fun-loving sort who whistles a great deal, was leading the party, but I bowed out, wanting to save my pennies but mostly because I wasn't feeling that sociable.

I spent the late afternoon alone on the Royal Pier. From there I could see the docks. Some kind of entertainment was under way. It had already gathered quite a crowd, young and old alike. A puppet show, I think it might have been. I refrained from buying a ticket, although I always love a good show. Instead, I chose a bench overlooking the murky strand to scribble a short letter home to my family on the notepaper I had just been encouraged to purchase. I didn't have much to say at this stage. I wrote, spurred on by pangs of homesickness more than anything else. Even though I hadn't much of interest to impart, I somehow felt it drew me closer to my folks to put the thoughts down and I knew that whatever lay ahead for me across this slate-flat sea, I was leaving a part of my life behind me forever and it felt vital to chronicle it. If I was deprived of my musical instruments with which to record my upcoming journey, then I was determined to have a go with words on paper.

My longing for my hard-working mother with her red-raw hands – she who had stroked and scratched a silent goodbye at my cheeks – expressed itself as a physical pain in my guts. In all my life, I had never told her that I love her.

In our London home we never resort to such declarations of emotion, but now perhaps I should. If I wasn't coming back... But my feelings were confused because I felt ashamed to even allow myself to think about Mother. I was a Man and a Man at War now. Still, I was fairly convinced that she would already be missing me too. As my dad would.

"Best of luck, lad," was the parting sentiment expressed by my father as he shook my hand. A man of few words and even less spared for me, his only son, only child. "Be sure to get yourself back safe. I'll be keeping an eye on that 'banjo' and the 'uke' for you. None but you can play the blasted things and your mother won't want them lying about, taking up useless space for nothing, and, never fear, I won't be giving away your job in the woodshop. So let us know how you are getting along and make it safe home." The longest speech he'd ever made to me.

I slipped in a brief description about the shipment of Indian wood I'd seen, then I sealed my news into its envelope. I managed to find a pillar box near the docks and slid my letter into it before we set sail. The knowledge that they would be receiving word from me within a few days lifted my spirits greatly.

*

Our crossing was uneventful and calm. It was a brisk night with a light sea breeze that smelt of diesel and freedom. I sat up on deck, legs outstretched, rolling fags, smoking, watching

7

the stars and the grey surge of water that looked black and impenetrable in the night, swilling and sloshing saltily against the hull. Close by me, a lantern had been hitched to a looping rope and it swung and danced with the movement of the ship. An occasional sailor passed by me, on his way to do this or that for the upkeep of our transport. Otherwise, I was a solitary soul grappling with the notion of going "abroad", leaving my own country for the very first time in my life. Maybe never to return. And about becoming a man, whatever that might mean. I attempted to write a tune in my head, a few chords that would express the contradictions I was feeling: excitement, fear, loneliness, inadequacy, a boyish dependency on home, adventure. I pulled out my whistle and blew a few breathy notes, but it was not so easy for me to compose music on a whistle. Aside from my family, I was missing my banjo, piano and ukulele more than anything else in the world. The tin whistle was about all I could fit into my kitbag and it was inadequate for my needs.

Who knows, perhaps I'll find a musical instrument to play in France? Wouldn't that be something.

*

We dropped anchor into the early morning harbour of Le Havre. It actually smelt foreign – pleasantly so. Beyond the port lay narrow streets inhabited by folk with unknown worlds and lives; folk with clogged feet whose paths I was unlikely to ever cross, but here I was staring at them, at the comings and goings of these different people. Disembarkation was scheduled to take a couple of hours. I and some of my newly made pals passed the time leaning against the ship's rail, smoking roll-ups. They had their eyes peeled for the young women. Who could spot the prettiest, was their distraction. Ginger, who is an odd-looking bloke with a face so very freckled, and whose hair tone is closer to dandelion than sandy, but who is gifted with the devil's own charm, seems to have an instinct for locating the loveliest of the ladies, that's for sure.

After a bit I left them to it. From the gently swaying boat that I suddenly felt afraid to leave, I listened to my first sounds of France – cries in a language I could not comprehend; a howling dog; the braying of a donkey, several donkeys; wooden cartwheels bumping and clacking against cobblestones; clopping feet; fishermen calling out their catch. One had a solid string basket full of writhing crabs.

Here I was hooked up to France, staring full on at "abroad", a strange country, and I was obliged to penetrate it whether I cared to or not.

We were given our orders as we disembarked, informed that our first duty was to report to our commanding officer who was waiting for us in a school up on a hillside beyond the town. The school, our temporary headquarters, was situated a couple of miles inland from the coast. These were my first footsteps on French soil. Ginger Green and

I set off together, keeping up a cracking pace, marching towards the building marked out for us with a red cross on a small, hand-drawn map allocated to every soldier as he alighted. Ginger is a couple of years older than I am but also a bachelor and a Londoner. He is from the East End and "proud to be an Eastender", playfully talking in cockney rhyming slang, while I am from Danbury Street in Islington. I asked him if he ever goes to the Hackney Empire. He said he'd been once or twice but that his all-time best theatrical experience had been hearing Marie Lloyd in January of last year singing to the troops at Crystal Palace. Ten thousand blokes were cheering her.

"*A little of what you fancy does you good…*" I crooned.
And:
"*Now you've got yer khaki on…*" I laughed.

I was glad to be in the company of a Londoner. I felt less homesick.

Ginger told me he is returning to the Front after a month of home leave. He said that "this war will be over by Christmas" is what the blokes were saying last year and the year before. It had to get worse before it gets better but he swears the troops have seen the worst of it now.

"We'll beat them this time round," he grinned, "and we'll be back home to see the snow, and you and I, I give you my word, we'll meet up for a few beers and a night out together at the music hall."

The thought of Ginger's promise really bucked me up.

*

A little about our daunting commanding officer whose name is Captain Miles Armstrong. He is exceedingly tall, taller than Ginger but more iron-rod upright, with earnest brown eyes and skin the colour of baking powder. His pallid complexion is accentuated by a strip of moustache – more a strip of black liquorice actually, which seems to be pinned precariously to his upper lip. It looks nothing like real hair and I think he must boot-polish it to make it so stiff and shiny. He seemed ill at ease in our company or he had given the same orders to too many infantrymen today. He wore a Webley Mark IV revolver in a holster on a belt round his waist, and he paced up and down the classroom, hands behind his back, all the while he addressed us.

"Private Stoneham."

"Yessir."

"You are new to this war?"

"Yessir," I said.

"Let me warn you that you will need every ounce of your courage. Bear in mind that there are soldiers: men, occasionally boys as young as sixteen, who are being court-martialled and shot by firing squad at the base camps for cowardice. The British Army does not look kindly upon cowards or deserters, have I made myself clear?"

This warning put the fear of God into me. Lord, I hope I can keep my courage up and not prove myself a wimp.

"Have I made myself clear, Private Stoneham?"

"Yessir."

"The omens are good. This should all be over soon and you'll be back to civvy life before you know it. Dismissed."

Ginger and Charley served under Armstrong last year. Ginger says Armstrong is a professional soldier. He takes no nonsense, despises all displays of weakness, but his bark is worse than his bite.

"At first, he'll scare you, but you'll get over it."

Will I? I am not so sure that I will. His threat of court-martial has left a bitter taste in my mouth. I am no hero. I am just a regular bloke who likes to sing and enjoy life and I know it.

*

Our billet is about six miles out of town. Several of us are sleeping in a hayloft belonging to a very whiskery French dairy farmer, whose broad-bottomed wife with her thin, high-pitched voice is hardly less hairy. It could be worse. At least it is dry and warm even if it smells of decaying hay, which is rather a sweet perfume actually. It's the rats that are giving me gyp. I am terrified of the blighters.

Myself and eight of the lads, including Ginger and

Charley, were given a pass and walked back to Le Havre to get ourselves an evening meal. Our pass was handed out with the proviso that we were back at our base and in our beds by eleven p.m. It is like being a kid again. Actually, my parents gave me more liberty!

During our search for hot food this evening, we wandered by the railway station, a rather impressive building with a fine glass roof. It is from there we will depart for the Front at some point within the next thirty-six hours, or so we have been forewarned by Captain Armstrong.

*

Today we were massed together in the school's yard. It was a hot day and we were in full uniform. Hundreds of us, spending our time square-bashing, seeing to our rifles and kit and preparing to move out. A part of the drill was bayonet practice.

"Bayonets at the ready!" yelled a flush-faced sergeant.

And onto our rifle clicks the seventeen-inch blade. Cold steel for close-quarter fighting. It is a chilling prospect, to be at such close range to an enemy soldier. Each of us infantrymen has been kitted with a .303 Lee Enfield rifle. The gun is fitted with a ten-round magazine which is easy to load, or it seems so here in the school play-yard, but when my fingers are trembling and some Jerry is shooting at me and my nerves are all over the place and I fear that I am a coward and know that whatever happens I must not make a run for it, I am not sure how deftly I will manage the reloading of it. The ammunition we are practising with here is useless. You shoot and it just fizzles, but Armstrong assured us that better-quality stuff will be on its way to us shortly. I sincerely hope so because what we have now wouldn't knock out a hamster. Our battalion, we are of the 17th London Regiment, has also been equipped with a couple of Vickers machine guns, but there are specially trained soldiers to operate those busters. You won't be catching me within arm's length of them!

*

In the evening we were permitted into town again. I think the leniency shown by our commanding officers is due to the fact that we are off to the Front and some of us might not make it back. The talk from those who have been there already is that it is grim. Mud, blood and more mud and blood. It rained this evening as Ginger and I and several others from our battalion trudged into town. I really fancied a bath, to wash some of the straw out of my hair and off my skin, but we couldn't find anywhere offering such a service. We found a music hall though, so paid a few francs – how much is that in real money? – and went in for a beer and a bit of jolly entertainment. I was dying to get up on the little stage and get my fingers on those piano keys. Instead, I sang my uniform socks off, joining in with all the songs I recognized even if they were sung in French, though a few were performed in English just for our boys. Those whose words I could not understand, I trilled and hummed to their tunes until my throat was hoarse, but I had a fun and relaxing time and washed it all down with a few pale beers. Do the French water down their beer? It is not of the same quality as British beer. It lacks the body!

Tomorrow we will be on our way to I scarcely know where. The Front. The prospect is both terrifying and exhilarating. What adventures lie ahead for us?

# HÉLÈNE

I am exhausted. So tired I hardly have the energy to wash and unpin and comb my hair. I have been mucking out the horse stable and scrubbing out the chicken coops. It was hot and dirty work on such a sultry afternoon. The chickens run freely during the day if the gates are locked but they are spending more time closed in. One went missing last week. Papa said it was stolen, for sure. Food prices are going crazy and people take desperate steps. There is no doubt that certain members of our small community are whispering that stealing from us Gastons is no sin, that we can afford to lose a fowl or two. And compared to some, I suppose we can.

My family are farming people. We also own a *petite auberge*. Our *auberge* is a modest-sized hotel, rather like a country inn that serves meals in its bistro. A bistro is larger than an *estaminet*, which is more like a bar that only sells snacks. Some of the British who stayed with us in the first year of the war said our fine establishment resembles an old English coaching house or hostelry. It is called *La Rose d'Or*. The Golden Rose. We live in the north of France in the *département* of Somme, in the region of Picardy, three kilometres outside the rather small town of Bray-sur-Somme. Our hotel sits right by the water, overlooking several natural lakes that flow from the Canal de la Somme. It is really pretty here. There are many streams and lakes around here with lots of ducks and herons and wildfowl and the area is quite famous for its trees and the wild plants growing along the riverbanks. In summer, in peacetime, my father and Pappy, my grandfather, like to go fishing. I prefer to go to the sea, but that is almost a day's journey. At the mouth of the river where the Somme runs into the sea, there are miles of empty beaches to visit and walk along. When I was a child, my parents would occasionally take us there.

All of our region is very tranquil and fertile. We Picard people are very proud of our rich farming heritage, or we were until two years ago when the Germans invaded our country.

*

I am seventeen. I finished school at fifteen, a week before the hostilities began on 28th July 1914. My mother had high hopes of me continuing with my education, but as soon as war broke out, my father announced, "Hélène, you are a grown girl now and we will be needing you to lend a hand."

Since then I have been assisting with the running chores of our bistro. Mostly, I wait on tables and serve the meals and I clean the dining room and kitchen after the diners have sloped off replete to their beds and my family, worn-out, is tucked up at the house sleeping. It's not the life I'd had in mind for myself, but during these difficult days the family needs to function as a single unit. It is the only way to survive. Maman, my mother, is well-educated. Grandma insisted on it. Maman was also a fine lace-maker and in local circles, at least, was a highly esteemed piano teacher, but now she is losing her eyesight. It is very sad. It is another reason why my parents need my labour, now more than ever.

*

We have rose trees and clematis climbing the exterior of our inn. Both are in flower at the present, but it is not as colourful hereabouts as it used to be. Two years of war and hardship with the Germans marching all over us and ripping our land apart with guns and shells and trenches, has leached the vitality out of our landscape, out of our hearts.

The River Somme, which flows right through our *département*, seems to be the focal point for the fighting. I am not quite sure why. Perhaps because the river runs all the way north to the sea?

The Somme and its wetlands hereabouts offer abundant supplies of delicious freshwater fish although, again because of the war, there is less fishing and fewer catches and parts of the river have been blown up, blocked off. In the good years, we had carp, pike, bream, eel and roach and, delivered to us from the Bay of Somme, the coastal region, we enjoyed fresh, naturally-salted herring. With all of these varieties, my father, who is our family chef and a master at it, created utterly delicious dishes.

Food is one of the principal topics of conversation in our household, partly because it is our family business, running both a hotel and restaurant, but also because everyone in our house loves to eat. Mealtimes *chez nous* used to be celebrations. However, our sources for food are fewer now that the Germans are in the vicinity. They confiscate all they can and they have blown up several of the bridges. The result is that some of our suppliers, who used to travel long distances to bring their produce to our local market, are no longer able to get through.

Prices are rising. Meat is fast becoming a luxury. Bread is twenty francs a kilo and flour costs the same. Papa bakes our loaves, but it hardly makes it more economical.

*

Still, even during these difficult years of battle, we count ourselves fortunate. We are more or less set back from the fighting. Even so, the Germans are too close for our comfort. The gun blasts we hear frequently are a sobering reminder.

We citizens hereabouts are all too familiar with the horrors of Occupation. We don't discuss the subject – it is too dangerous – but you can see the concern and fear in the eyes of residents.

Two years ago our community had a near escape when our little parish of Bray-sur-Somme was conquered by the Imperial German Army, but thank goodness, we were liberated relatively quickly. We were "occupied territory" for only a brief spell, although those summer weeks were drawn out and oppressive.

Here is how it happened: in August 1914, a few weeks after the war had begun, the German Army invaded and, within no time, captured Bray. However, they were quickly pushed back by our valiant French troops. That autumn was very distressing. I hate to recall it. Expelling the Germans involved the bombing of some of our local buildings. The result was that a number of homes and workplaces were damaged and several citizens were badly hurt. However, the assault pushed the Germans back, sweeping them off our doorstep. We were quiet for a while. Until last year, when they attempted to recapture our town. On that occasion, they shelled St Nicolas church, on the hill just off the main square. Their blasts damaged the bell tower and shattered the stained-glass windows. (Our region is well known for the art of stained glass.)

The church is very ancient. It was built by Benedictine monks on the site of a ruined monastery and in earlier centuries was quite famous for its six bells. However, during the revolution in 1789 five bells were taken and melted down to make money!

Nonetheless, our *clocher massif*, our bell tower of St Nicolas, with its one remaining historic bell has been a classified monument for the past eight years and the town was very proud of it. Some of Bray's more religious inhabitants were doubly outraged by last year's assault. Not only was this an invasion, they cried, it was also vandalism aimed against Catholicism. "Next, the Germans will be shooting our priests as they have done in Belgium."

I thought this reaction was rather dramatic because many of the Germans are Catholics like ourselves. Until one morning, while I was sweeping out the bistro, I overheard Monsieur Balitrand, our mayor, discussing the subject with Papa. They were partaking of an early morning cognac as is their habit. Cognac, hunting and heated debates on the daily topics in our local newspaper, *Courrier Picard,* are what bond most of the men in our town.

"Would you credit it," growled *le Maire*, "the Imperial German Army has been executing the priests in every Belgian town they have invaded. Killing them as they pass through." He was stabbing his finger at a page lying open on the zinc bar in front of him.

"Better not let poor old Father Thèry see that," replied my father, pouring more cognac. "The old fellow has not been in good health since the church took that battering last year. I do believe the business of the bell tower shook him up rotten. He took the matter personally."

\*

In my opinion – not that anyone was asking me – in fact, I think neither man was aware of my presence in the room – it is not possible to hide information from Father Thèry. He is like a dog rummaging for buried bones, digging up everything around him. He knows everyone's affairs better than they do. He asks loads of questions whenever he is invited by Maman and Grandma to our home for a glass of wine, a meal if he is lucky, and he is always begging a few centimes for the upkeep of his service. Even when I go to confession, before he gives me the prayers for my penance, he quizzes me about everything on earth. The Saturday before last he warned me against dallying with French soldiers in the street. What a cheek! But I was kneeling in the confessional box and could hardly talk back to a holy father, even an old busybody like him. I rarely speak to the French soldiers unless they come into the bistro for a beer. One of them stopped and asked me directions to Corbie and while I was pointing out the route, Father Thèry stepped out of the church. I saw his beady eyes glance in our direction and knew he'd think the worst of me.

Still, as I said, every day we count our blessings and help one another wherever we can. Even the silly old farts of the community.

# DENNIS

At eleven last night, we said farewell to Le Havre. The train blew its whistle, jerked and jolted forwards, throwing us all against one another, and then it chugged merrily out of the station, full steam ahead. It was a bit of a squeeze in our carriage, one hundred and fourteen of us squashed up together. I wished that I and several others (I won't mention names) had got that bath we were so badly in need of. I slept a bit as the train trundled east towards Germany, towards our destination, wherever that might be. We have not been told yet. Our commanding officers remain as inscrutable as ever.

I was rather taken aback to see on the platform at Le Havre, waiting to be loaded, stacks and stacks of rifles, crates of ammunition and several big guns. New guns, lined up ready to go.

"Blimey, look at all that. Something big is in the offing," I heard a fellow from another regiment remark.

At about one in the morning, I was overcome with one of my ever more regular bouts of sickness, a dread of what lay ahead – the sight of all those guns and rifles and ammunition had set me off – and I had to push my way across to the window while the others slept and snored through the lurching, rocking night. I was heaving but could not vomit. It was nothing but a dry, impotent terror.

I leaned against the glass, smoking roll-ups – several too many! – gazing out at the ghostly shapes of the countryside partially lit by the moon. I was silently calculating how far away I was now from London as I hummed…

*Singing songs of Piccadilly,*
*Strand and Leicester Square,*
*Till Paddy got excited,*
*Then he shouted to them there:*
*It's a long way to Tipperary,*
*It's a long way to go.*

Each of us has been supplied with an identity disc so that our families can be notified if anything happens to us (dog tags, the blokes call them). *We never know when our time is up*, I was thinking, still humming, *and if I have to cop it for King George I'd rather do so back in Blighty surrounded by my family and not by the smells of black tobacco and stewed, oniony rabbit. And these French eat horse meat.*

*Goodbye, Piccadilly,*
*Farewell, Leicester Square,*
*It's a long, long way to…*

*

*Amiens*

The train drew to a halt in a great cloud of steam and we were ordered to grab our kitbags and disembark. Last stop for us. I jumped down onto the platform and was hit by the welcoming aroma of breakfast, French style: the early morning baking of soft, warm bread and coffee freshly brewed. I have always been a tea drinker but right at that moment I could have been persuaded to accept a cup of that thick coffee the French all drink. It is very dark and strong. Some of the fellows have told me that this is not real coffee. There is no coffee to be had these days. The stuff they are boiling up now has a base not of beans but of a plant called chicory, but I wouldn't know the difference.

Outside the station at Amiens, we were ordered to prepare to march to our waiting positions. Amiens looks like an interesting city, the little we saw of it as we passed through. It is perched on the banks of the River Somme. Ginger explained that at the start of the war over two years ago, Amiens was the Advanced Base for the British Expeditionary Force and was captured by the Germans in the last week of August in 1914, but the French claimed it back a month later and it has remained in the hands of the Allies ever since. Corporal Masters pointed out that it is strategically important to us, the Allies, and our main objective here is to keep Germany from advancing in this direction. The station was impressive with lots of glass and on our way through the city to the river, which we followed for a while, we passed a monumental Gothic church. The city's cathedral. It is totally different to our St Paul's in London. This one had lots of heads and figures staring out from it, which I found a bit spooky. I wouldn't want to be locked in there alone for a night. Once we had all gathered at the water's edge, a sergeant who I had never seen before yelled out our orders. "Right, lads, get marching. Eyes to the east."

And so we began to forge forward, four abreast, with our laden kitbags on our backs. Left, right, left right… Ginger was waving at everyone as though he were returning home. He's a funny bloke. Makes me laugh. I like him and feel safer when I'm in his company.

# HÉLÈNE

I have just returned from the market and unloaded my basket of the few bits I could haggle for. Horse meat was yet again the best from a stall of meagre choice. Thank heavens we have our own eggs. Milk was a price. At this rate, we will have to dilute it. Still, I must not complain. In some towns not too far from us, in Péronne and Pozières, for example, the Kaiser's soldiers are living amongst the French citizens. Wherever they gain a foothold, they requisition homes and move in themselves. Then they steal all the food, leaving our French neighbours to go hungry. Papa says that in some villages, the French are having to queue for bread, even at 20 francs a kilo, while the invading armies help themselves to whatever they fancy, plundering precious ornaments, family heirlooms and paintings. Further to the east, close to the Belgian border and into Belgium itself, the Germans have gained control. Living under an adverse military is horrible. The eastern French and Belgians are starving, very afraid and rather cut off from the rest of the nation. All their horses for working their fields have been confiscated and, sometimes, the Germans shoot citizens in the street, killing them because they have hidden *their own* food in their cellars or for disobeying unreasonable German orders. So, we are indeed fortunate, even if there are no luscious pork chops for dinner.

*

Our closest city is Amiens. It is also the capital of the region and is such a pretty city of red-brick houses and stone mansions with a splendid Gothic cathedral, Notre-Dame. It is twice the size of Notre-Dame in Paris. I used to enjoy visiting Amiens with my parents, strolling by the Somme, listening to the tolling of the bells, but we rarely if ever make the journey these days. It is safer to stay home. You never know what will happen while you are out.

Currently, Amiens is overrun with British soldiers. They have made it a base station, a headquarters, and they pour into it by the thousands every day by train. Most people don't mind them because they are our allies; fighting on our side. At the market this morning, Monsieur Ladèlle, the butcher, who yells about everything and is permanently red in the face, was carrying on about the foreign soldiers being everywhere in the vicinity now. He said they are quite decent and most can be trusted, although where will we find the meat to feed them all, he was moaning. Our mayor speaks well of them too. He says that the principal differences occur between the governments, not the ordinary people. The British and French governments don't always see eye to eye on how this war should be won. He says we need the Americans if we want to "get this damn business behind us and get on with our lives".

My father insists we look at events from a positive perspective. He claims, and he is right, that the British and colonial soldiers are bringing business to the region. They have money to spend, particularly those from Australia and New Zealand. The pity for us is that last year we closed the hotel and, aside from the farm, we are opening the restaurant only in the evenings, because there is a limited choice of menus to offer our clients. Our *auberge* has always been very proud of, and a little bit famous for, its duck entrée: *pâté de canard en croûte*. Also, in late autumn and winter, the Golden Rose serves yummy game stews, roasts and pâtés, but these delicious plates are rarely on our *cartes du jour* these days. Grandma makes the best thick and creamy pumpkin soup in the world, which is a firm favourite with the mayor, whom she likes to spoil. She says it is not because Michel Balitrand is the mayor nor because he is president of the regional hunting association and therefore a very important man. It is because she has known him since she was a girl. They both attended the local school. Perhaps she had a crush on him. That would be funny. He is not as handsome or hardworking as Pappy, but he is quite powerful in local circles.

Since war broke out, *Monsieur le Maire* has allocated far fewer hunting permits.

"We need to keep the food in our own hands," he tells my father. "And we don't want every blasted fool wandering about the woods with a gun. Things are bad enough as they are."

My father, of course, owns a hunting rifle and is a fine marksman. Pappy, too. Game meat is an important source of our protein, especially now, and rabbit stew with onions is a household favourite.

# DENNIS

So this is it, is it? The Front? I am in the middle of nowhere surrounded by wetlands, lakes, villages. Well, I am not yet in the trenches nor have I been installed at a base camp. We have arrived on the outskirts of one of the many small towns set back from the Front Line and here we are to stay until we are called to fight. It is very rural, predominantly farming land, though I couldn't say what they are cultivating.

We had to stand in line while the sergeant, the same bloke rallying us all in Amiens, told us where we were to be billeted. It took over an hour to get to me. By then, I was exhausted. I'd had too little sleep and was gasping for a cuppa.

*

Our advance from Amiens this morning took a little over three hours. For some of the way our progress remained within sight of the river and then we cut up to a more northerly path that led us through villages and agricultural landscape. If we saw anyone, they either waved a welcome or just ignored us. No one was hostile. Geese and chickens were picking their way across the streets and we passed plenty of farmers riding donkeys, transporting small loads of hay or fire kindling. I like the houses here, built with slender red bricks, all with slatted wooden shutters. I wouldn't mind having a go at crafting some of those shutters. Every now and then we came upon a house that was all stone and very grand. The landed gentry, I suppose.

It was a hazy morning and grew hazier the closer we got to our destination. At first the countryside was all flat and rather boring but then, after we had passed through a town called Corbie, it grew a little hillier, but not steep.

By my reckoning we are close to twenty-five miles distance from the city. Directly to the east of it, I believe. I know we are more or less south of a town called Albert. Funny that. Why would they, here in France, call a town Albert? My granddad is Albert. He was christened after Queen Victoria's husband. I didn't know foreigners would want to call themselves or their towns after our Prince Albert.

*

I don't think I ever paused to ask myself what "Front Line" actually means or what it represents. Its official title is the "Western Front". And what is that? I had not tried to picture it, which is possibly a very good thing because it might have scared the wits out of me if I had known what I was getting myself into.

Corporal Masters explained to me that the Western Front crosses through the rolling chalk downs of the province of Picardy to the marshy valley of the River Somme and the

Canal de la Somme, which is where we are located now. I can see the Somme River or its canal as I write, steaming tin mug of tea at my elbow. It was the Germans who created the Western Front. It runs in a zigzag fashion for about five hundred miles from the northern borders of Belgium, descending south to where France meets Switzerland and consists of a series of deep trenches inhabited by thousands of soldiers. Platoons and regiments camp in the trenches and stay put with their weapons and rations at the ready, awaiting orders to shoot or attack. Both sides have dug trenches. The point of the exercise is to stop our enemies taking our trenches, because if they do, they can cross without hindrance into unoccupied France and keep advancing. Our job, emphasized Corporal Masters, is to keep free France in the hands of the French and, if possible, to overrun the German trenches and, with the use of guns, grenades and bayonets, capture the German soldiers guarding them. If we can occupy our enemy's trenches we are gaining ground, winning back territory the Germans have already conquered.

Frequently, soldiers are ordered to climb from their trench, cross a strip of land known as "No Man's Land" and invade their enemy's trenches and dugouts.

Conditions are very basic, Masters warned me. Well, I will soon see it for myself.

The men who are back from the Front, resting in

villages east of where I am staying or nearby hamlets and settlements, all look exhausted. Some appear shocked or haunted, as though they had just seen a ghost. One or two will exchange a word but little more about what they have been living through. Most don't talk about it. Two English blokes who have been given some trench leave are billeted in the same barn as I am. Both just stare with blank faces into the middle distance, smoking.

It's unnerving.

I do not intend to write about any of this in my letters to my parents. I will have to make sure to keep a fairly light-hearted tone so they don't worry. I will concentrate on describing the countryside and requesting they send news to me. What's playing at the Chapel on the Green, I wonder, or one of our other local music halls? Whoever's on the bill, they'll be singing the latest tunes. I wish I was there to sing along with them.

*Take me back to dear old Blighty!*
*Put me on the train for London town!*
*Take me over there,*
*Drop me ANYWHERE,*
*Liverpool, Leeds, or Birmingham, well, I don't care!*

Oh, blimey, I do miss home.

# HÉLÈNE

We live in a rambling, nineteenth-century red-brick house with numerous corridors and rooms and fireplaces. It is set behind tall, rusted iron gates at the end of a driveway. It has a large front yard and there are stables off to one side. The property is about one hundred and fifty metres along the street and round the corner from the *auberge*. Easy walking distance and ideal for us. It needs plenty of cleaning and, unfortunately, these days that is also part of my workload.

My parents were given the house and its surrounding apple orchards by Maman's family before Maman's illness, when my grandparents felt they did not wish to maintain the property for themselves. It was on the understanding that they continue to live with us, which has proved to be the best thing for everyone. The house has four storeys and is so spacious that even with five of us living in it – six before my brother, Pierre, was called up to fight – the fourth floor and, above it, the attic level are never used for bedrooms. Up on that fourth floor is a world full of boxes. Grandma's boxes. I long to know what she keeps in them, but I have never been allowed to go beyond those locked doors. One of the rooms on that floor is known as the "sewing room" and contains dozens of neat piles of coloured materials and strips of lace and a black Singer sewing machine embossed with gold. There is also a big square wooden table dressed with a green velvet cloth. Maman used to disappear up there in the afternoons to do her lacework, after her piano classes were over for the day. Frequently Grandma would accompany her and turn the sewing machine. Grandma stores reels of cotton and threads of silk in the machine's wooden base. The two of them would stay ensconced there for hours, forgetting all worlds beyond their own, and I would jealously creep up the stairs, trying hard not to tread on the creaky wooden steps, to eavesdrop. I would hear their laughter like the tinkling of many small bells and I'd hear the cranking handle of the sewing machine as it turned and bobbed and vibrated and I burned to know what confidences they were sharing, what made them so light-hearted. Was it the sewing, the lace-making, their creations, or was it other more dangerous secrets? Romantic secrets. Secrets Father Thèry would give his eye teeth to know.

Whenever I enquired, my grandma would reply, "Women's stories, dear girl," with a finger tapping her nose and a gleam in her eye, "and little girls have no business being nosy or asking too many questions."

Ah, but those days are long gone. Buried in our memories. And I am no longer "a little girl".

These days, we concentrate on existing and working to keep the *auberge* from closing down. I am a young woman now, but I rarely catch or am invited into the world of tinkling laughter.

Papa and I work hard every day to make the bistro welcoming and keep it bustling with customers. Maman is no longer capable of the cooking. The last time she tried, she burnt her hand badly so Papa forbade her to come anywhere near the stoves again. She enjoys arranging the vases of flowers though, most of which she gathers from our very big garden or along the lanes and down by the lakes. Grandma prepares the vegetables for the kitchen and makes all the sauces while Pappy husbands all our land. This is hard toil alone because it includes all our crop fields, my grandparents' orchards and the vegetable gardens. He is up at the crack of dawn and goes to bed early, so we don't see so much of him these days. It was easier when Pierre, my brother, was here to lend a hand with the spadework and ploughing, but Pappy never complains. He is very strong – indomitable really – and good-natured and spends all his days hoeing and planting or harvesting and when he is not out in the fields, he is with his pigeons. For years he has kept carrier pigeons. One of his great delights is to send one of his birds to a dairy farmer in Meaux with an order for cheese. It is always a moment of triumph when the farmer travels in this direction and makes a stop at our bistro to deliver us several great wheels of creamy Brie packed in straw in wooden boxes.

Everywhere smells of cheese for days afterwards.

We have no livestock, no cows or goats of our own, so we have never made our own dairy products. We have a sizable acreage though, on which grow the apples in my grandparents' orchards, sugar beet, wheat, peas, potatoes and corn. Since this horrid war began, a wider variety of fresh vegetables have become more difficult to source. We are fortunate to own so much farmland. My Pappy is too old to be called up as a soldier and my father, though younger, has a special exemption because Maman is going blind. This means we have manpower to till the fields and we can grow almost sufficient produce to service our bistro and our domestic needs, although, as I said, the choices are limited. Still, everyone understands and nobody complains. People are happy to eat a decent hot meal for a few francs and to sup one or two glasses of fairly drinkable house wine surrounded by good company.

I believe that offering companionship plays an important role in our success. Papa goes out of his way to create a friendly ambience, particularly for those who live alone. Whiling away an evening with other members of the community is far preferable to sitting at home worrying about the advancing Front Line. Papa knows the residents who are a bit hard up and he doesn't mind if they just come along and sit at the bar all evening with the same glass. He is a kind and generous host and people really like him.

*

We own chickens, ducks, a horse and a donkey, and we have a fine black dog, a Beauceron. His name is Renard, which is French for fox, but he doesn't look one bit like a fox. He has a short-haired, black-and-tan coat and is sleek and tall. Quite aristocratic, I like to think. I am not quite sure why we christened him Renard. I think it was my brother's doing. Anyway that's his name now and Renard seems perfectly happy with it. He is an excellent guard dog so if the Germans come to our door, I would set him on them. As I have no brothers and sisters now to keep me company, Renard is my best friend.

Well, I do still have my brother somewhere. Pierre is four years older than me but he went off to war over two years ago and we have heard nothing from him for almost twelve months. In the beginning, he wrote occasional letters to my parents, and once in a while news of him was brought back from the Front by fellow soldiers. It sounded as though he was fit and keeping his spirits up, but all has gone quiet now. The silence and the uncertainty add a terrible strain to Maman's diminishing health. It is another reason why, even if I was given an opportunity to leave home and go to Paris to work or study, which I do surreptitiously dream of, I could not abandon my family. Not now, not yet.

Still, if I am honest, growing up to be a young woman

at this time in France's history on the outskirts of a tiny provincial town is a bit dull and rather lonely.

We are thirty-four kilometres from Amiens, which is west of us, with its lively city life, but it would be unthinkable for me to make a day trip there. It is as inaccessible to me as Paris, the capital, one hundred and twenty kilometres directly south.

I am perfectly capable of travelling alone. I have been riding since I was six and am a skilled horsewoman. I even drive the wagon and have frequently brought in the hay bales. Once Pappy has lifted them onto the wagon, I steer them home safely to the barn. But I would never be allowed to travel to Amiens, not without my family. If my brother were here to escort me perhaps it would be different.

And, of course, there are no handsome young farmers to take me dancing or invite me for walks along the riverbank. All the young men, like Pierre, have been conscripted and sent to the Front to fight for France. The French soldiers who have stayed in Bray seem so serious, concentrating on nothing but the war. A few English-speaking soldiers have begun to frequent the bistro, but why would any of them notice a country serving-girl like me?

My grandma calls me frivolous for allowing myself to dream of dancing and romance at a time like this, but I believe she has forgotten what it was like to be young, to want to have fun, to be carefree and know excitement.

But one day, when these hostilities are over, our lives will surely be better. There will be laughter again and, who knows, perhaps a flirtation or two.

# DENNIS

I have been in this makeshift dormitory for over twenty-four hours and still have no orders to move to the Front. I heard on the grapevine that a big offensive is being planned and we are to be involved in that at some point. Very little information is given to us. I am not sure if even Captain Armstrong knows precisely what is going on. If he does, he is certainly keeping mum about it. We haven't seen too much of him. The officers are not billeted with us. They have other quarters, frequently in one of the posh houses, staying with families. Us ordinary blokes get the barns and the livestock sheds. I am kipping in a barn. One of the blokes with me, Harold Beaker, is also from Islington. He lives in Upper Street – just round the corner from me! How about that? He is sleeping in a cow byre while I have my quarters up in the loft where the hay is stored. I reach my "bedroom" by climbing a handmade wooden ladder, firmly held together with some sort of string. I lie on my bed of clean straw, play my tin whistle, thinking up tunes and wondering what lies ahead. It is a waiting game and a bit unsettling.

*

Day six here and not a great deal happening. Many of the infantrymen seem to be resting. We have not even been summoned for drill practice nor do we have very much of anything to do. I hate the idleness, this hiatus. It strikes me as curious after all the ammunition and weapons I saw being transported here.

The talk is that new trenches and deep tunnels are being prepared, made ready for a large-scale attack, although I have not received this information officially. There have been trainloads of miners arriving from various parts of Britain. They have been brought in because they are experts at tunnelling. It is hoped they will blow the guts out of the German trenches from beneath the earth's surface. And then we can all go home.

It could all be gossip or idle chatter. It is impossible to get a clear picture. I am feeling out on a limb, cut off and definitely homesick, so I have been taking myself off for a few long walks to have a butcher's and see what this country is all about. The villages hereabouts are built partly of stone, but mostly of the red brick I noticed earlier. I quite like those I have strolled through. I don't know if it is because we are out in the countryside and not in a big city like London, but the old men and the girls and women – there are no young men – always give a wave or nod of their heads, but in spite of their acceptance of us, the region itself has a bleak mood about it, a heaviness, although I suspect that it is more to do with the fighting than the general atmosphere or any unfriendliness intended by the natives.

For the most part, it is a flat and rather dull region, with mile after mile of fields. Even now in midsummer when it is hot, if the wind gets up, it blows in from the east across from occupied Belgium and howls through the main streets of the villages. In most of the villages, the main street is the only street. Leading off from that main artery are dust tracks and narrow passageways where chickens wander about freely, clucking and scavenging. There are plenty of children running to and fro, squabbling and screaming or carrying heavy loads of farm equipment on their backs. Often they are in their bare feet, and some of them call out to me, "*Bonjour, Tommy.*"

Charley says the French call all Englishmen, "Tommy". I did wonder why they were assuming my name was Tommy and not Dennis.

This morning I saw a group of the local women all in white bonnets, pinafores over their long dresses and wooden clogs gathered at *le lavoir*, which is a communal, outdoor laundry house. There they have fresh running stream water. The roof overhead is built on timber pillars, but there are no walls. They were chattering and gossiping like budgerigars as they worked, bending and rising, sleeves drawn up, slapping the garments as though punishing them. Their raucous laughter rang out around the wind-bitten countryside and it was very cheering to hear. I would like to be able to engage them in conversation but I cannot speak a word of the language. Well, I have learnt "*bonjour*".

*

Everybody in these villages seems to work non-stop. They are not sitting about idle, not even the nippers, yet everybody looks half-starved. Two years of war has cost them dearly. When the Germans get a grip and occupy a town, it seems they confiscate anything and everything that takes their fancy. The French call it stealing, but the Germans consider it their right as they are the occupying force. They even appropriate the crops from the fields and the French are obliged to hide whatever they can in cellars, behind false walls, built in between the houses. If they don't, they starve. This region, a finger's width from the Front, is not occupied and that is what we are fighting for: to keep it French, to drive the Boche back. Boche is a French slang word meaning stubborn, obstinate or hard-headed. It also means Kraut or German, and it is not a compliment. Everybody here hates the Germans. They spit on the ground at the very mention of the enemy.

*

My battalion has been split up here, there and everywhere for the purposes of housing, although we are all within a sturdy walking distance of one another. I am still billeted in the same spacious draughty old barn. I am guessing that it is about ten miles behind the Front Line and on the outskirts of a big village. The village has a hyphenated name that I cannot pronounce. We are within earshot of the guns so there is no forgetting that there is a war on. Big guns booming distantly, nothing like the rifles we are carrying with our kit. The shots sound like continuous thunder or someone waving a giant, buckled sheet of metal. I have heard that sound at the blacksmith's place back in Islington. Here, it is much louder, more menacing. It bores into you, rumbling away at your confidence as though you were being shaken by an invisible force. Night is the worst. A full-volume blaring that makes the barn tremble. I lie awake shivering, unable to sleep, afraid of what lies in store for me. Am I a coward? Will I be shot by a firing squad and disgrace my family? Are all the rest of the blokes sleeping or are they as scared as I am? I am not hearing the snores of peaceful dreaming, that's for sure.

*

We have now been told that we will not be in the first wave of the attack, which is due to begin within the next few days and which our seniors are promising will be the biggest offensive of the war so far. We are to wait back, staying here in this reserve position. Our orders will be given to us as soon as. As soon as what? I have no idea. Many of the blokes are keeping diaries, writing letters, reading books, keeping their minds occupied. It is the hanging about that is driving me up the wall. Those who are not new to this war lark, seem more at ease, less jittery. I have no idea whether all the letters are intended for posting or just to keep their nerves steady, like confiding in a silent friend when you have so much fear coiled up inside you, you think you might burst. I can't admit to being scared, can I? After Captain Armstrong's warning in Le Havre, I won't be confiding my faint-heartedness to anyone. I don't want to face a firing squad.

*

Ginger came looking for me at lunchtime. I was mighty pleased to see his friendly face, whistling as he strolled up, hands in his pockets as though he was on his way to Hyde Park and hadn't a care in the world. "There you are, Den!"

He wanted me to join a party. He and Charley, along with a few Aussie soldiers and one or two others from a Lancashire regiment, were heading off to a bar on the outskirts of the little town where we are billeted. I really fancied an outing but I was a bit reticent about joining them. I kicked my heels, a little embarrassed, not wanting to refuse and be rude, to be judged a prude.

Some blokes probably feel they have to squeeze their entire life's experiences into the short time that might be left to them. I'm not really like that. I know that we can't count our mortal days even in peacetime but given the death toll here, the likelihood is that our lives will be short. Very short indeed. Days or, if we are lucky, possibly weeks. I sincerely hope not, even so…

Ginger was puzzled by my silence, my lack of enthusiasm. "What's up, mate, why don't you want to come along? I thought you enjoyed a good laugh."

No one wants to die a virgin, but…

"Sorry, Ginger, but I just don't fancy spending my evening in the company of … the company of well, you know…"

"No, Den, I don't"

"Good time girls. I suppose I am a bit of a romantic when it comes to women."

I didn't admit it out loud, but I am waiting for the girl of my dreams to come dancing into my life, and wherever she is, whoever she is, she will have to love music or she'll be no girl for me. A country pub on the River Thames with some lively musical entertainment is my style of a great evening out. All the more reason to stay alive and get myself safely home again.

Ginger laughed out loud at my concerns. "Good time girls! You are a card, Den, you really are. The Golden Rose is a little eatery on the water a couple of miles outside the town. Some Lancashire lads had a meal there and raved about it. Charley and I went back with them a couple of nights ago. It serves home-style cooking and the family have tucked away some decent house wine at ten francs a jug. And more to the point, the waitress, a voluptuous brunette, is a bit of alright," winked Ginger.

It sounded inviting and I felt a bit of a fool with my silly assumptions so I accepted Ginger's invitation to join the party. It would get me out of the barn for a bit and stop me brooding.

# HÉLÈNE

Maman and Papa and my grandparents are all sleeping now. It is very late. As usual, I stayed up to clear away the dishes from the tables, wash and dry them and then sluice the surfaces and scrub the café floors in preparation for business tomorrow. It has gone two in the morning and I am quite exhausted, but in the best of humours. A group of British soldiers were in again last night, but this time it was a larger turnout, about ten, and mostly new faces. I think word of our *auberge* must be spreading. I am sure all these servicemen are not staying in our town. They must be travelling from further afield to dine with us. It is down to Papa's cooking and friendliness, I have no doubt.

This last evening was extra special because one of the young men discovered Maman's piano. We have had it covered beneath a cloth and locked away for over a year. I am not quite sure how he found it because it was neatly tucked out of sight behind a heavy velvet curtain. We have closed off a section of the dining area in the bistro. Since the war began and with food rations being short, Papa decided it was wasteful to keep the entire place open when we don't have the business to fill it. Mind you, if the soldiers start coming in numbers, we may be obliged to open it up again.

The private who found the piano must have been looking for the lavatories. Anyway, he seemed so excited by his discovery that he came hurrying, almost jumping, to ask whether we would mind if he had the key and, if so, might he play a few tunes? It has been so long since anyone put fingers to that keyboard that I had to run about all over the place and then up the street to the house to find where Maman had hidden the key.

When he and I unlocked it and he ran his fingers across the notes, it was still in tune, which was a miracle. The soldier, who is British, I think, requested the use of it. I was a little uncertain because I thought it might upset Maman to know that someone else was playing her precious instrument. She had followed me from the house to the bistro kitchen, "to collect a plate of food," she said, but truly I think she wanted to know what the excitement was about and why I had been after the key. It was the unmistakable sound of piano chords that caused her face to light up. I saw her stop and listen, the furrow on her brow disappearing as her face broke into a smile. She recognized the sounds of her piano, but who was playing it? No one aside from her in our household has ever taken an interest in music, which saddens her greatly. Alas, I don't have a musical bone in my body though I do love to dance. Maman set aside her supper plate and stepped towards the door that leads into the public section of the bistro. There she hovered. Her eyesight is too poor for her to make out anything more than shapes and shadows a distance across a room. She was puzzling. Who was sitting on the stool over at the keyboard?

I bumped into her as I made my way to the kitchen to hand in an order and to refill a small carafe of house red.

"Hélène, who is playing my piano?"

"It's one of the British soldiers, Maman. Do you mind?"

"*Mais, non*. He plays well. He lacks a certain technique but he performs with feeling and natural aptitude."

I hadn't really been paying any attention to the quality of the foreigner's accomplishments. I was happy to hear the room resound with song and I was very aware how it had elevated the mood of the diners, both French and British. For a brief moment, it was reminiscent of the old days, a pre-war atmosphere.

"Describe his features to me?"

By this time, I was in the kitchen, handing my father the dinner order I had just taken and reaching for the house red wine. Maman had followed me.

"Whose features?"

"The young man playing my piano."

"I didn't notice, Maman. Please, Maman, move over. I must serve these two dinners and this carafe. I haven't paid the pianist any attention."

52

"Do you recognize the music? Is it a popular British tune?"

I was back at the door and she was worrying at my arm. I thought I might drop the plates.

"Please, Hélène, turn around and look across the room. Is he handsome?"

"Goodness, Maman, I can only see his back from here. What does it matter? He is hunched over the keyboard…"

"Ah, a man in communion with his playing. You do not see that so often. In my years of teaching, I probably only found a handful who were so in harmony with their music. He must be handsome, I am sure of it."

Maman has grown a little foolish since she began losing her sight, or so Papa says. I say that she has become excitable but also romantic and she buries herself in Nature in a way that I never noticed when I was smaller. She hears sounds I think she was never aware of in her previous life. "Do you hear the birds, Hélène?" she calls to me when she is in the garden. She spends a great deal of time in the garden now, working with the roses. "Listen, the turtle-doves are cooing, singing their love songs to one another, calling across the courtyard to their companions." Also, she listens to the carrier pigeons my Pappy keeps. She swears she can hear them signalling to us as they return to their coops.

I tell her, "Maman, they are just birds, that's all!"

"Just birds? Your grandfather's pigeons are shopping for us, Hélène. That is a rare feat."

Because she has always loved the piano and taught music to primary school pupils, her ear has always been finely tuned, but since her sight began to fail, her hearing seems even more acute. She lives through a world of sounds and scents, seeming to communicate with and through them.

"Hélène, are you paying attention to me?"

"Sorry, what did you say?"

"Please ask the English soldier to play *Le Temps des Cerises* or *Au Clair de la Lune* for me."

"Do you think he will know those songs? I don't think he speaks any French, Maman. I'd feel awkward asking."

"Everybody knows them, pet. And when you go over to request this of him, please make a mental note of what he looks like. Be observant, ask him his name and where he is from and then, later, you can recount to me every detail about him. Later, when our diners and the British have gone home, I want to picture how the man playing my piano, and playing it so well, looks."

I sighed and nodded, served the hot dishes on my tray and then I made my way over to the far side of the dining room to the piano. The soldier was taking a pause, chatting to one of his comrades, a tall fellow with a wild head of yellowy-red hair who I think has been in here once before. He was leaning against the piano, smoking a cigarette.

"*Bonsoir*, excuse me," I said.

The tall gingery fellow swung round to face me. The pianist, also.

"*Bonsoir*, I am Hélène Gaston; welcome to my parent's bistro."

The piano player was grinning at me, smiling and grinning, if you could say it was possible to do both at once.

"*Parlez-vous français?*" I asked him.

He shook his head, still gazing at me. He had blond curly hair, more corkscrew than curly, cropped in military style, of course, and piercing green eyes.

Maman has taught me to speak some English. Not as well as she converses in it, but I decided to pluck up my courage and try it out. "*Ma mere*, my mother, has requested, please, you play *Le Temps des Cerises*. Do you know it?"

He shook his head again and laughed. Such a warm open laugh.

"You speak good English, miss. Unfortunately, jer parley par fransays," he replied with an excruciating accent and such misuse of grammar that I also burst out laughing.

"Hélène! Hélène!" My father was calling me from the door that leads to the kitchen. Papa looked harassed with a white serviette thrown over his shoulder as usual, his sleeves rolled up above his elbows and perspiration from the heat of the stoves sprouting all over his face and balding head.

"*Je viens, Papa*. Excuse me, please," I said to the soldiers, "I have to go."

"Wait! Name, what's your name? *Comment vous namez?*" called the blond one at the piano.

"Hélène, you fool," nudged his comrade. "She introduced herself to us a couple of minutes ago and her father has just called her. *Bonsoir Hélène, moi nom ist Ginger.* My, you are awfully pretty."

I suspect that the one who calls himself Ginger is a bit of a flirt, but I rather liked the blond-haired musician. He is handsome, and plays the piano well even if he seems a little ill-at-ease and rather shy.

I hope he returns to eat in the bistro. I believe he will come back because he seemed so excited to find a piano in a war zone.

# DENNIS

I barely glimpsed the lovely young lady again. For the rest of the evening, she was hurrying to and fro, serving at the tables, carrying and lifting, working far too hard for such a beauty. I longed to go over and carry some of those plates to lessen her loads. And so, on an impulse, I did. I swung away from the keyboard and made a dive for her to swoop the plates from her elegant arms and, guess what, four dirty dinner plates went crashing to the floor and smashed to smithereens. It silenced the room. If I had wanted to draw attention to myself, I couldn't have made a better job of it. I sank to my haunches, pulled out one of the handkerchiefs I'd bought before boarding the ship in Southampton and started wiping the floor. Gravy all over the hanky while gathering up the shards of china.

A family of French at one of the nearby tables was laughing in a mocking way at me, calling me "*rosbif*". I was red as a beetroot, I could feel the flush in my face. I had so wanted to impress and help this beautiful Hélène. Hélène. It was hard to feel a greater fool. Perhaps she also perceived me as a "roast beef", a derogatory nickname the French use against the British. They see us as lumps of overcooked English meat, but even if Hélène saw me in that light, she was soon on her knees beside me. The nearness of her, the scent of her – a pine soapy scent along with cooking smells all mixed in together – made my head swim. With every fibre of my being I wanted to touch her, to lay my hand on her skin, to feel the warmth and the softness of her. It troubled me so, I felt tears well up into my eyes.

"I'm ever so sorry, miss. I hope you've got plenty more where they came from. I'm glad though that table had finished eating. They'd all but cleaned off the plates, hadn't they? A hungry lot. All that good cooking, of course. My, Ginger's spot on. You are breathtakingly pretty."

"Please," she said in English with an accent so sweet you could not dream it. "Don't worry. I don't understand all your words, but you have tears in your eyes. Please, don't cry. It's fine. It saves the washing up," and then she laughed.

She has sea-blue eyes. She is not only beautiful but gracious with it. I think I have lost my heart!

*

The good news is that there are two public wash houses in this little town of Bray so at some point I can get properly cleaned up. Most mornings I have to strip off and wash at the pump. Other days, I am pulling up pails from the well on the farm where I am billeted. No such thing as heating the water on a hot stove. No, we line up and wash with cold

water and it is very hard to get your bar of soap to sud –
soap comes wrapped in brown paper and is part of our kit
rations. Thank goodness it's summer. Let's hope we are all
back home with this war behind us before winter sets in.
I wouldn't fancy doing any of this in the snow. I sang as I
washed, suds or no suds. My head was full of the beauty of
that lovely girl in the café.

*

I had been longing to go back to the Golden Rose last night
but at five in the afternoon, my battalion was called together.
Captain Armstrong informed us that we were still not listed
to go to the Front Line yet. Not today anyway. I cannot say
if I was disappointed or relieved. Part of me wants to get on
with it, get the war over and done with, and another part of
me is dreading everything about it.

Several other regiments were given the order to get ready
for a roll call at seven this morning. An offensive was due to
begin an hour later and we were all to be marched to base
camp. The roll call did include us. Some of the fellows I met
were colonials. One or two others had sailed from South
Africa. Several I spoke to were excited at the prospect of
fighting, saying if you have to do it you might as well be in at
the Front, doing your bit to the full extent. I don't have that
courage and frankly, when I thought about it, I was bloody
glad not to be amongst those front-liners.

While we wait for the order to advance, we have

been allocated other chores. This morning I, along with approximately five hundred or so other blokes (men not exclusively from my battalion), marched in the early-morning sunshine a fair old distance along a road flanked by fields of soaring corn. We met the sun rising higher in front of us as we moved east. We were on our way to a base camp. Approaching from the opposite direction, came a light traffic of carts and wagons driven by farmers, smoking their pipes, chivvying their beasts, minding their business as they transported their cargoes or labourers. To a man, they paid little attention to the platoons of soldiers transgressing their country territory. Our boots were falling and rising. Clump, clump. The sound like percussion. Clip, clop from the mules pulling the carts. Drumming of feet up, feet down, arms swinging, in unison. I started humming – feet up, feet down, and then I broke into song. A few chords later, Ginger, now whistling, and Charley who were alongside me fell in and then a few others and before you knew it we were all in harmonious early-morning voice, lifting the roof off the clear blue sky.

*We are Fred Karno's army, we are the ragtime infantry.*
*We cannot fight, we cannot shoot, what bleeding use*
*are we?....*

Even the birds in the plane and poplar trees were cawing and chirruping, adding their pennyworth.

*Pack up your troubles in your old kitbag,*
*And smile, smile, smile...*

"Louder lads," I called, like the leader of the band.

*...While you've a Lucifer to light your fag,*
*Smile, boys, that's the style.*
*What's the use of worrying?*

Ah, there is nothing quite like a rousing sing-song, is there? This ditty sounded so different out here in the open air, compared to when I first heard it at the Bedford music hall in Camden Town. Ah, Camden Town. My dad bought me my piano in Camden Town. But that was last year, before I was in uniform. Now, when you're marching along, four abreast, scents of the summer countryside in your nostrils, men behind and in front of you, sweating in the sunshine, all with the same fears and the same determination to win this bloody war for King and country, it certainly boosts your spirits.

Well, for a short time it cheered us and then we passed three officers standing about, overseeing a small party of British soldiers, "Sheffield battalion", Charley said, digging positions for four guns in a sloping green field. It seemed an odd exercise. What were they intending to achieve there? It was not the first time I asked myself whether anyone really knows what is going on here.

*

Once we had reported in at base camp, we were ordered to await the arrival of a transport vehicle carrying ammunition. I then learned that the town of Bray-sur-Somme is a munitions dump. Frankly, it struck me as pretty dangerous to be storing live ammunition in a populated zone, even if the population is sparse. I was disturbed, but I kept my troubled thoughts to myself. Bray must be running the risk of an attack by Jerry, who will want to blow up our explosives and sabotage our depot. Are the local inhabitants aware of all this? I am glad for that pretty girl Hélène and her family that the Golden Rose is a few miles out of the village, along the riverbank. Thinking of her sent me off into a dream. I hope I can get back to her café again soon. A pretty girl and a piano. How fortunate is that?

My name was bawled out, breaking into my reveries.

"Private Stoneham!"

I jumped to attention. "Yessir!"

I was one of several blokes ordered to assist with the unloading of the anticipated shells and bullets. There was an entire consignment of Number 5 Mills bombs coming through. These are hand grenades. Every soldier is to be allocated two.

*

While I was standing about, waiting for the transport corps to show up with the consignments of ammunition from the town, I had a thorough scout around. This was the closest I have been so far to the actual fighting. Being there gave me an opportunity to see how this trench system was being organized.

From here, to access the lines of fire, communication trenches have been dug. These lead you to the back-up and then the front lines. The corpses and the wounded are also returned by this route, if they can be brought back at all. There were several medical orderlies working at strategic points, greeting stretcher-bearers, organizing the placement of the wounded as though they were rows of traffic, calling to nurses to take pulses. I spotted two nuns and a padre in a wide-brimmed black hat wandering to and fro, bending over men on stretchers, muttering prayers, I suppose, or words of encouragement. There were dozens and dozens of men on stretchers. I could hardly believe it. And still they kept arriving. Some were upright, or partially so, being dragged or hauled by other exhausted, filthy-looking soldiers. The less wounded were helping others more gravely injured. Several I spotted had lost limbs. There was a short queue of ambulances waiting in a line, but insufficient for the numbers of wounded men constantly being delivered from the fighting. Two soldiers close by me, both still conscious but evidently in pain, were talking about the hell of crossing

No Man's Land to invade enemy territory. Running with their guns and bayonets at the ready, praying they would not be shot down. Evidently, their prayers were partially answered. They had been hurt but they were not a-gonna.

As the morning gave way to high noon and the day crossed over into the afternoon heavy with clouds of acrid smoke, I had the distinct sense that a rising panic was setting in. As though the news from the Front was not good.

"What's happening?" I called to a soldier who careened by me. He did not stop to answer, possibly did not hear or understand me. There are blokes from all over the world fighting this war, it turns out.

As vehicles departed for makeshift hospitals being established in the towns, other ambulances parked up and another fleet of young nurses poured out of them. I don't know where they are from or where based. They were caring for the wounded, of which there were hundreds, with such calm and diligence. Some of the soldiers, when they had been patched up, were sent back to fight. One young blond nurse who sounded as though she hailed from Yorkshire came across a stretcher with a German soldier lying on it.

"Ooh, look who I found," she called to anyone who might be listening.

I shuffled a little closer. I have no idea whether the Jerry had been collected up from the war zone by mistake or had been taken prisoner, but he was bleeding. He had been shot in the thigh and our medics took as much care of him as they did our own men. He looked bloody terrified, but the Yorkshire lass nattered away to him light-heartedly, trying to put him at his ease. My teeth began to chatter as the reality of all that I was seeing began to sink in. I caught sight of Ginger. He was surrounded by a bevy of attractive, laughing nurses and was regaling them with stories, charming them senseless. English girls and colonials. He behaved as though unaware of the pandemonium that was escalating all around us.

It was impressive to see young women facing these atrocities with such calm expressions and businesslike manners while I was stunned and battling against vomiting. I suppose these girls are trained for all this. Even so, their positive energy was an example to me because I had never imagined that I would be witnessing such carnage: loss of limbs, body parts missing, men moaning and bleeding.

"We need more ammunition!"

"Call in replacement regiments!"

Oh, Lord, would this be me to the Front? I asked myself when I heard a lieutenant comment on the lack of men still active at the Front.

Selfishly, I also realized that if not today or tomorrow then some day soon there will be no escaping my turn to go to the Front, to face what all these men had endured. There will be no flinching, no shirking, no squirming my way out of it.

Or if I do, it will be execution by firing squad.

"This is why you are here, Dennis," I said to myself. I was just rolling a fag when a consignment of weapons finally arrived and I was called to assist with the unpacking.

"Quick, lad, jump to it!" Some sergeant I had never seen before was yelling at me. "We need this equipment to the Front at the double. Men are being mowed down out there!"

Everybody seemed to be in a rush. Did they all know what they were doing?

It was impossible to tell.

*Dennis, you have been living in a bit of a bubble, strolling about the villages, meeting Hélène, entertaining people on the piano.* It had rather turned my head and I was beginning to forget the reason I had been sent here.

This realization shook me up.

While I was smoking my cigarette, one of the blokes I was working alongside suddenly got the call: "Your company will fall in, ready yourselves to go to the Front Line".

"Yessir."

My blood went cold because at first I thought the officer was talking to me, but it was an American they were addressing. I'd been chatting to him for about fifteen minutes as we unloaded the stacked rifles, sharing a joke. I recounted details of the Golden Rose, invited him to come along with me one evening, to have a beer and a sing-song. He was a Yank from the suburbs of New York, he told me, but he had been living in Paris since 1912, studying to be a painter, and he was fighting with the British Army. The US are not in this war, not yet anyway. He listened to his orders, made no comment, gave me a nod and then carefully passed the shells he was cradling over to me. "Catcha later, buddy. Nice talking. We'll have that beer at that bar together soon."

"You betcha," said I. I would have given him a slap on the back except my arms were full. "Best of luck, mate."

"Sure," he said and disappeared amongst the chaos of men arriving and departing.

I sincerely hope he has the best of luck.

*

What a horror. The day was a disaster, a bloodbath. A minority came back alive and those that did were calling it a "bloody circus", "to hell in a hand basket".

Up out of the trenches the soldiers had scrambled, bayonets at the ready, hurling themselves directly into No Man's Land. Then down onto their bellies, crawling forward, moving like lizards. All the time they were being shot at, targeted by grenades. Some of the colonial regiments did grand stuff and got into the enemy trenches, took prisoners and hauled them back. Hundreds of prisoners. It was chaos trying to deal with all the Germans who had been arrested, some of them ripped to shreds and bleeding like our boys. I don't know where they will be holding them all.

And there was me, still at base camp, feeling useless and

unequal to the task. I thought we would be staying out there, but after we'd unloaded some guns and wooden boxes of stuff, witnessed the results of the day's events, we were sent back to our original billets, yet again to await instructions.

It was a slow march home.

*

Ginger, Charley, Harold and I along with an Aussie private we've met called Jackson, who was fighting at Gallipoli before they shipped him and his regiment here, returned to the Golden Rose bistro again last night. I looked for the Yank to invite him along but didn't see him anywhere. Ginger said all those at the Front who had survived the day's events would probably still be in their trench. The talk was of nothing but all that we had seen and heard at base camp. This latest offensive, which was planned to defeat or at least knock back the Germans did not go as intended. Thousands of men were killed at the Front today. The morale amongst the troops is said to be low. I will surely be posted to the Front any minute now.

That might explain why all the blokes were hell-bent on getting out for the evening, having a few too many drinks and a good time. This could be our very last beer.

I confess my reasons for accompanying them were definitely more amorous than for the company or food. Like all British low rankers, my pay is a mere sixpence a day. So I cannot afford to be spending my army wages on dining out. I can stretch to one beer in a bar of an evening, but now that I have set eyes on Hélène, as long as I am posted in the vicinity, I don't think I will be able to stay away. She is a magnet, too powerful to resist. The trouble is there is only one Hélène and I am guessing that I am not the only recruit who is sweet on her. Ginger has a twinkle in his eye when he sees her, that's for sure, and she'll probably prefer a chap who has a little bit of experience with the girls, rather than a callow little carpenter and musician like myself. I was hoping Ginger might have gone sweet on one of the nurses he was chatting to this morning, but if he has invited any of them out he hasn't mentioned it to me. And who knows, Hélène possibly has a sweetheart. She is far too pretty to be single and not fought over.

Jackson told me that the rankers from down under, the Australians and New Zealanders, are earning far more than our blokes. They are on about six shillings a day for their war efforts. Ten times my pay! So they can spend far more time in the bars and bistros than I ever could. Jackson bought me a couple of beakers of wine at the Golden Rose, which was very decent of him. I explained I don't have much with which to return the gesture. He didn't seem to care.

"No worries, cobber," he said to me.

"Cobber?" Did he mean cobbler? Such a curious language.

"You're the entertainment, mate. You play well, kid. That's good enough for me."

"Thanks," I said, but I don't like to sponge off anyone, not even cobbers (whoever they might be) and I would hate for anyone to think I am cadging off them. I prefer to earn my keep or stay away, but how can I stay away from Hélène? I am thinking I might suggest myself as her family's resident pianist while we are in this neck of the woods. I'll earn my dinners, or a glass or two of wine, and I'll be close to Hélène at the same time.

*

One of the British fellows drinking at the Golden Rose at one of the other tables last night turned out to be an expert on British folk tunes and Morris dancing. He went by the name of George and, when he'd had a few, he mapped out the steps to the Morris dance for all those who did not know it, to get to grips with it. What an evening we had of it. I got on the "ol' Joanna" as Ginger calls it, which is to say, I played the piano, and a bunch of grown men in uniform, released from the horrors of the Front for a few brief hours, took to dancing. Some took the role of the girls. One or two swiped off the tablecloths and wrapped them round their waists, like skirts, skipping and wiggling their hips. It was a hoot. The French locals watched on in amazement, incredulous, and then Harold Beaker strolled over to Hélène's mother, who is short-sighted, I think, and asked if she would accept his hand and take to the floor with him. She looked a bit embarrassed at first, but her pretty daughter – what a pretty daughter; I can barely take my eyes off her – gave an encouraging nudge to her mother and off the dear lady went into the centre of the room. Guided by Harold, they began to glide about the space. Delicate as clouds, the pair were. She looked like an angel. I can see where Hélène gets her looks and grace from. The customers, all locals except for our lot, eventually picked up the mood and shoved the round tables on which they had been eating or drinking to the sides of the room, creating a dance floor. If I had not been at the keys, I would have asked the girl of my dreams to take a turn with me, but Ginger beat me to it. I knew he was keen on her. I could see it in his eyes. In any case, I was the music-maker and couldn't let the lads and the crowd down. That's show business!

I walked home elated at having got my fingers back at the piano and to the joy built up from all the music-making. I am proud to say that we took the roof off that place, and I couldn't sleep dreaming about that girl, Hélène Gaston, with her long, chocolate-brown hair.

*

We had to cut across fields this morning to reach the base camp. The roads are chocka with ammunition and supply traffic. We weren't singing and some had hangovers. I was debating with Ginger about meat.

"The French eat horse," I said. "I've seen it on sale in a butcher's, great slabs of dark-blooded hanks of flesh."

"Fancy that," he teased.

"They won't get me tasting it."

Ginger replied that we have eaten it already and I did not know the difference. I think he was pulling my leg, unless it was in Le Havre. If so, he's right. I didn't spot the difference.

"They boil it up in the dixies," he said, "and serve it as our daily hot provisions. They cook the meat for so long, you wouldn't know what you were chewing. It all tastes like soggy curtains so what does it matter?" he insisted.

I wasn't going to argue with him. I don't feel like arguing with anyone and I don't feel like going to war. I just want to go back to the Golden Rose and drink in Hélène's smile.

We remained working out at the base camp and our daily rations were served up there. "Death-by-Dixie" some of the blokes call the food. A "dixie" is a cooking pot and it could well be bubbling with horse meat. It smells revolting.

*

I spotted the American fellow I was unloading shells with a couple of days back. He was brought in on a stretcher.

"Hello there! Remember me, mate?" He didn't answer. "How are you doing? We'll have that beer soon, eh?" I was trying to be encouraging, but he didn't look too bright.

He stared back at me with glazed eyes and then he slipped away. Just like that. It was so silent, without even

72

closing his lids, so suddenly, almost secretively, as though he wanted no fuss. Alive one minute and then just a corpse the next and still staring at me, like a fish on a slab. I could have bawled my eyes out at his loss, as though he were my own brother. Even though he had never told me his name.

That's war for you, and here was my first personal encounter with death and I was fighting back my tears like a kid. You get attached because you are bonded in duty and unpalatable tasks and because you witness sights you don't want to talk about to anyone else. You are incapable of talking about to anyone else. There is a collusion, it seems to me. You become a silent witness.

I am not capable of discussing these experiences with anyone, nor of writing about them in letters to home. Nor would I want to share the sights I have seen with Hélène even though she is a neighbour to the war, a victim of it. I do not care to worry those sea-blue eyes of hers or cause her pain.

# HÉLÈNE

My father sleeps in the afternoons. We work so late and start so early that Papa needs his nap. He disappears for a few hours after the soups and stews have been prepared, while Maman and Grandma are locked away together, talking or sewing. Maman, of course, can't sew anymore but she and Grandma still spend their afternoons together, sometimes out in the garden or the courtyard when the weather is as fine as now.

Dennis has asked me to go for a walk with him. If I ask my parents' permission, I doubt they will grant it.

It would be quite simple for me to accept a walk along the river with him without anyone in the family noticing I was gone, if it was an afternoon promenade. My family wouldn't be pleased. I know they like him because they have said so, commented upon what a gentle young man he is and probably unsuited for military work, but I don't think it has occurred to any of them that I am attracted to him. He makes me laugh and laughter is in short supply these days. I cannot allow myself to grow to like him too much though because I have no idea how long he will posted here, near Bray. He could be gone already and I wouldn't know, although I do think that he would try to get a message to me if he was ordered to move on.

# DENNIS

I invited Hélène to take a walk with me along the riverbank and she accepted. I could hardly believe my good fortune. She brought her dog with her. A big black fellow. Black and tan, he is, a bruiser of a beast! Pretty fierce. I suppose her parents thought he'd better be her chaperone in case I didn't behave myself. She calls him Raynar. I think that is his name, but whenever I called him, he got down on his haunches and growled at me.

Poplar trees. I like them. This seems to be a region of poplar trees. They line some of the roads here, very straight roads that Hélène said were built by the Romans hundreds of years ago. The poplars are tall and narrow and cast long shadows into the fields. They fit well here, flanking roads that lead on forever. To where? To Germany, I suppose. I am not sure I have ever seen poplar trees in London. Perhaps they don't grow there? I wonder what their wood would be like to carve. I don't think I have ever heard Dad mention it.

Hélène had brought a paper package of cheese, salami and *baguette* (I really like these long French loaves) and we sat by the lake, within the shade of the poplars, legs outstretched towards the water, happily munching our meal. It was the best ever. At one point, Hélène spotted a water vole digging about at the water's edge.

"*Regardez*," she pointed as it slipped away out of sight, "*c'est un campagnol terrestre.*"

The setting was perfect even with her dog trying to steal my cheese.

Then a grey heron lifted itself from a split tree trunk semi-submerged in the green water and flew away, streaking like a comet. The day was magnificent.

I would like to come back in peacetime and perch myself there on that bank of the Somme River and do some fishing, with Hélène at my side recounting stories of her childhood.

London seemed so far in the past but I wanted to share it with her, bring it to life. I talked far too much though because I was a bit shy in her company. I nattered on about a café in London where I used to go and eat, very different from her parents' establishment. Manze's in Chapel Market.

"It opened in 1902," I said to her. She looked puzzled, concentrating hard on following what I was telling her. I grabbed a stick lying on the grass on the bank where we were seated and I drew the figures 1 9 0 2.

"The owner is a friend of my dad's." I was talking slowly and a bit too loud. "It would be the ticket to take you there, Hélène, introduce you to London food. I remember going

there with my dad when I was a boy. This tall I was."
I jumped up and drew a line across my thigh and Raynar
grabbed my salami, which slipped to the ground as I rose.

"*Quand vous etiez un jeune garçon.* When you were
a young boy," she said. She was reassuring me that she
understood.

"Yeah, when I was a kid, it was always a big treat.
Sometimes when we had to go to order wood," I slapped my
hand against the trunk of a nearby tree, "wood," I repeated
"for Dad's business, we'd make a stop at Manze's and get
ourselves some pie. There was always a man outside the
shop with a barrel of live eels. He'd take them out one at a
time and then cut them up for Dad or for anyone who was
ordering a pint of eels. Those market days were really lively.
Men walking about selling horses, yelling out the cost to buy
a horse."

"They also have markets in London city?" She seemed
surprised.

"'Get me a horse, Dad, will you?' I'd tease. I used to
fancy myself on a horse. Mum always bought her veg at the
market. Well, she bought what we didn't grow down on our
allotment. After the family outing to the market, Dad always
went for a pint at one of the corner locals – the pubs – and
Mum would go home to get the dinner ready. Dad took me
along with him and I'd be bought a tall glass of sarsaparilla
and told to wait outside the snug door, but the barman

78

always winked and called me in with a wave of his big arm, thick as a leg of lamb it was. When the longed-for beckoning finally happened, I scooted inside, plonked myself on the shiny wooden bench at Dad's side while he jawed away to his pals, barely aware of my presence. I listened in, loving the atmosphere and watching Dad. All the while, I was guzzling on my drink, which was sticky and delicious."

"Is that your best memory, your most treasured memory of home, Dennis?"

"No, the best moments were when Dad would say, 'Give us a tune, lad, sing us a song, Dennis, my boy. This boy of mine has got real talent,' he'd boast and I was that proud, Hélène. I'd be on my feet in no time, strumming at my uke."

"Uke?" Hélène shrugged. "I don't understand this word, Dennis."

"Ukulele. Musical instrument. I always took it with me, on the off chance Dad'd ask me to give his pals a tune. But whenever I broached the subject of wanting to play professionally, to take to the boards, make my living in the music hall, he'd bark at me that I was being fanciful, that the music hall was no life for a real man. 'Cut out the dreaming, Dennis, my boy. You'll be a carpenter just like me.' And if I worked real hard, he'd say to cheer me up, 'You might just make a master carpenter, Dennis, one day.' How I miss my home and my folks, Hélène."

I had got carried away with my memories and was

suddenly drawn back to the present and how Hélène was gazing at me with those wide, serious sea-blue eyes.

"Lord, did you make sense of any of that rambling? Sorry to talk so much. I wish I could speak to you so you could understand."

"Yes, please, Dennis, continue to speak to me. I understand many things of what you tell me. Many things. Eels who swims like fish, I understand this. We have eels under the rocks here," she smiled. "*Les anguilles.* Upriver near the sea. *La mer.* I like to listen to your voice. You have a beautiful voice, Denniz."

Denniz, that was me. Her pronunciation of my name triggered joy within me. I grinned at her, at life, at the possibility that I was Denniz and not just a scared, insignificant soldier. And it was Denniz who burst into song.

*"If you were the only girl in the world*
*and I was the only boy*
*Nothing else would matter in the world today*
*We could go on loving in the same old way..."*

And then I fell silent. I hadn't forgotten the lyrics. I knew them by heart. This song was the big hit of spring while I was still living in England. My mouth went dry because I was thrown off kilter by the words "*loving* in the same old way".

Loving. Love. It seemed so unlikely. It was a miraculous gift in the heart of brutality and war. Here I was, sitting on this Somme riverbank, peacefully, staring into the eyes of this beautiful, beautiful girl. Only then did it dawn on me that I was helpless. I loved this girl. This girl I was sitting alongside who was calling me Denniz. I wanted to take her in my arms and kiss her hard, but I knew that would be improper so I lifted up my hand to her cheek and gently stroked her face.

"You are wonderful," I said. "I want to take you home with me."

We walked and we talked to each other and we listened even when we didn't really understand what the other was saying. It was like mining for gold. How we both jumped up and down and giggled with a sense of victory when we hit upon a story or two we could both relate to. Most of the talking that was achieved was done by Hélène because she can express herself a fair bit in English and she understands more than she speaks, but I am lost, hopelessly lost in French.

The rest of the time, our little outing was conducted in companionable silence.

"Wood," I kept repeating, trying to say how much I like the poplars. I wanted her to understand that my dad is a master carpenter but that was too difficult. In the end I stood on the grassy bank acting out the business of cutting wood, miming making a chair until she fell about laughing. *"Ah, bois, vous parlez des arbres. Le bois des arbres? Votre père est un menuisier."*

*"Bois.* Does that mean wood? Clever girl, you understand everything. When I return here, will you come out with me again, please?"

And would you believe it? She nodded and grinned.

I love her!

# HÉLÈNE

I sat out in the courtyard with Maman and Grandma this afternoon, warming ourselves in the sun beneath the trailing yellow roses. We were shelling peas. Usually it takes us several days to shell our harvest but not this year. Food is definitely scarcer and with all the English and colonial soldiers travelling in and out of the region, we have far more mouths to feed. I was fairly silent most of the time, dreaming about the young English soldier, Dennis, who sings and plays the piano. I was singing in my head, *"If you were the only girl in the world."* I was playing over in my mind moments from our promenade.

Maman and Grandma were teasing me about my silence and dreamy eyes and guessed it must be because of him. It set Maman nattering to Grandma about all kinds of gossip from their younger days.

Until two of our neighbours, Madame Thibaud and Madame Cheron, dropped in to pass the time of day with us. They are both middle-aged and live in small adjoining properties down along by the lock, not far from where Dennis and I walked yesterday.

Madame Thibaud wore her sandy hair caught up in a yarn snood. Both were wearing muddied and scuffed, laced work boots beneath their coarse skirts even in the heat. They had hiked down the lane for a chat and for a bit of female company while they worked and had carried on their shoulders two heavy sacks of beans that needed topping and tailing. I was sent in to find chairs for them both. While I was inside in the dining room, I could hear the babble of their conversation. The pitch had risen feverishly but when I stepped back outside, the four women were all silent, concentrating on their busy fingers dipping in and out of the hillocks of green vegetables.

As I sat down, all four women watched me closely.

Had these two old biddies seen Dennis and me together? Was that what they were gossiping about while I went to collect chairs? Might tittle-tattling be the reason for their unannounced visit?

Suddenly, Grandma was reminding the other three of the romantic betrayal of some woman who had lived in our town, a woman I had never heard of. Maman recounted how the woman had been abandoned by her lover who was a "foreigner" and how she had spent the rest of her days pining for him, awaiting his promised return, which never came about. According to Maman, she ended her life as a broken-hearted, disillusioned spinster.

Was this an attempt by a cunning quartet to warn me

away from Dennis or was I being too sensitive and overly suspicious?

Madame Thibaud, who had lost her husband in a farming accident before the war broke out and has not been of entirely sound mind since, or so say my family, recounted a story in dramatic hush-hush tones as though there were people peering round the corners of the house, busting to listen in on her conversation. I bent my head low trying not to snigger. The tale was of a young village girl from hereabouts.

"Who?" commanded Grandma.

The widow refused to name names. On she went. "Then the girl found herself in trouble and…"

"In trouble?!"

I did not understand the gist of the piece but the others "oohed" and "aahed" and shook their heads in shock. Madame Thibaud warned that her tale was not to be repeated to the men of the household. "They cannot understand the weaknesses of the heart or any depths of emotions. They cannot face what we have to do, not with the same sanguinity as us women," she bragged.

"It's true," concurred her neighbour. "Men know nothing of the real world. They only understand the land and the rearing of pigs. A few exceptions, if they are bright, can talk business, but I never leave the deal-doings to Monsieur Cheron. You can never trust what a man tells you and above all, you must never believe what they promise you."

Madame Cheron then turned to me and in front of the others asked me outright, "Have you a beau, Hélène?"

I was taken aback, flustered. All hands went still, peas and beans inert in skirts like expired fish.

The pig farmer's wife pursued her busy-bodying further with another question. "Possibly one of those Tommy fellows who comes to eat in the bistro? They seem a carefree bunch with a few francs to throw around. Is there one of them who takes your fancy, girl?"

Silence. The women leaned forward. Four faces watching me intently, as though the fate of the war depended on my answer.

"No," I declared softly.

"I'm glad to hear it," smiled Grandma. "When this war is over, you'll soon find yourself a nice, decent Frenchman."

# DENNIS

Finally, my turn came as I knew it had to. We were given our marching orders, shifting to beyond the town of Albert and then directed east. We were holed up in a communication trench for a day or so and then brought forward to the firing line. I cannot pronounce the name of this stretch of trench. We have been here for several days now.

One of the blokes from our battalion, not anyone I have met or even seen before, spends all his spare time sketching the scenes around us. His pictures are gory. Who would want to remember all this but, then again, who could ever forget it? I have seen corpses everywhere, littering trenches or in dugouts, lying out there on No Man's Land beyond the barbed wire.

Our commanding officer, Captain Armstrong, blows a whistle, a small silver whistle inscribed by its maker, J Hudson of Birmingham, to give us his orders, to send us up out of the front-line trench, to wriggle our way out under the barbed wire on a charge towards the enemy who then mows us down like skittles. Sometimes, we manage to progress to the next trench, or we are forced back. I haven't infiltrated any Jerry trenches yet.

In the midst of all these seemingly chaotic advances and retreats, while we await the shrill call to action of Captain Armstrong's whistle or for our next order to be yelled at us – to shoot, attack, lie low or whatever it is going to be – I take out my own tin whistle and I play a tune or two. I am attempting to keep myself cheerful, or at least from going mad. Our enemies are the shells, shrapnel, bullets, the mud and the rats. Some of the rats have tails so long you think they could strangle you. I don't know which scares me the most: the Germans or the rats. Sometimes I natter for the sake of it, to keep myself from going crazy. I talk to whoever else is nearby me and still alive or just to myself. Gibbering away like a loony. This morning I fell into conversation with some soldiers from Australia. Friendly blokes, and not snooty. They were reminiscing about back home and their journey over here from Melbourne, which is way down under, across the world. Like Jackson, these blokes are colonial soldiers although they prefer to call themselves ANZACs, which stands for Australian and New Zealand Army Corps. Some of their stories are incredible. Well, if I am feeling homesick, what can it be like for those poor blighters? Most of them haven't seen their homeland or loved ones in over two years. They were fighting in another country far from here before they got the order to help out in France. Gallipoli was where they were, in the Dardanelles. Some were then posted to Palestine. I haven't a clue where these places are and half of these fellows didn't seem too sure either. What they know is that it was just as much a bloody mess there as it is here.

Chiack. Now there's a word I've never heard before. It's Aussie talk, one of them informed me, and means to tease someone, to take the mickey out of them in a kindly way. "Hey, Dennis, we are just chiacking, cobber. We're teasing you, mate."

Their accents are so thick. I suppose it sounds like Ginger's cockney talk to those who are not used to it. Half the time it is impossible to understand what the colonials are saying. It's certainly not English they are speaking and might as well be frog language.

*

I think about Hélène. Oh, how I yearn for Hélène. Her beauty is a miracle to me in the midst of all this stinking putrefaction. I go over our conversations time and again. She makes me laugh. I talk to her when I am not talking to myself or my neighbours. I write her letters and I write letters home.

*

We have stores of rations to keep us going in an emergency and food is brought to us when and if the catering corps can get rations through. Six-ounce tins of corned beef. I never thought that the sight of corned beef, bully beef, we call it, could get my taste buds and juices going so. Hélène laughed about me calling our meat rations "bully beef". She said that is an anglicized term for *boeuf bouilli*, which is French, she says, for boiled beef. Our tins don't taste like any French food I have eaten, particularly at the Golden Rose. I wonder who is at the Golden Rose now, who is eating there, asking Hélène for a dance or taking her walking. Ginger? I haven't seen Ginger for a couple of days. I was thinking about him earlier, looking out for him, remembering our conversation about horse meat. Nor Charley. Where is he? I hope to God they are safe. They are my brothers in war.

*

Crouched in this trench, I suppose I am no more than 180 yards from Fritz (that is another of our nicknames for the Germans), who is crouched in his trench, probably as scared and uncomfortable as we are. They sent us a tear shell earlier today. That was my first taste of gas and pretty horrific it was too, although I was far from the main thrust of the thing. After it came whizzing over, we bunched down and then scarpered as best we could along our earthen pen. Like animals, all hunched up, trying to escape the fumes and the smoke and dust, scrambling through the chaos. Then there I was, stumbling over bodies, three bodies, soft and floppy, crumpled on top of one another. Three lads, all dead. I was too scared to look at their faces. In case I recognized them. And then I did. I had to fight not to be sick. I had been talking to one of them earlier this morning. He showed me a picture of his girlfriend, Ethel, back home in Sunderland. I told him I'd met a French lass, a lovely girl, and that I wanted to take her back to London with me.

"Me and my Ethel's getting married in the autumn when I get me leave," he told me proudly.

I pity poor Ethel now.

Suddenly, in the midst of all this pandemonium, the whistle blew and we were given the order to stop everything and charge. Stop everything? We are trying to breathe some clean air is what we are doing, Captain, so as not to suffocate on the ruddy gas! We were ordered to fix on our bayonets – oh, how I hate that moment of clicking on the blade – and get ready to fight, get ready to cross the neutral zone, under the barbed wire again, to attack Jerry again, which we did. Braving it like true British soldiers, through an area that resembled dirty cotton wool there had been so much shelling. I could see guns going off in the not-so-distance ahead of me, flashing and glittering, like rows of sequins on the frocks of the singers at the music halls. They are aiming at us and that includes me. By God, I was trembling, shivering with fear. I have never been so afraid, not simply for the loss of my own life though certainly that too because I am no hero, but more specifically for the sights we might face and what I had just seen of Ethel's dead fiancé.

I spotted men with their heads caved in and brains spilling out. There were rats too, feeding off men's flesh, but

I am not going to write about the rats. Big black bastards with tails as thick as skipping ropes. Too awful.

I started to sing. At first I was singing and humming just to myself to keep from blubbering like a scared baby. I was mentally calling on Hélène to give me strength, that her smiling face would get me through this, praying that this was not the day I was to die...

*"If you were the only girl in the world*
*and I was the only boy*
*Nothing else would matter in the world today*
*We could go on loving in the same old way..."*

But then I raised my voice and belted out the tune into the daylight, draped in grey clouds of dust, and the bloke next to me took up the lyrics and then another fellow further down the line and before I knew it we had a chorus going. We were a desperate, charging choir. We had the faces of sweated men, grimed with earth and trauma. Our eyes were whiter on account of our soiled flesh and the fright was there in our look, but we sang our lungs out because we all had a girl somewhere, be it a mother or a sister or a lover. A girl that we wanted to live to see again.

I changed the words.

"Come on, sing loud, lads."

*...We will go on living in the same old way. We will go on living in the same old way...*

And some of us made it. Some of us. The rest are dead in that field, but they went down singing.

*

Ever since this afternoon, I have been thinking about my mother, dear Florrie. I can hear my dad calling to her now.

"Pour us a stout, Florrie, there's my gal."

I have never thought of it before but they are a love story, the pair of them, my folks, in their quiet London way. Friday nights, a drink at their local on the green. Then a few eels and whelks from the stall on the corner, rounded off with a smoke. Once a year an outing to the races with Dad's sister, Clara. All dressed up in their best. Salt of the earth, my family is. I want to get out of here and see them again and let them know how much I appreciate them. I want them to meet Hélène and tell me that they love her as much as I do, and that she's salt of the earth too and that she'll take good care of me when we're married, like Mum cares for Dad.

I'd kill for a plate of eel pie and mash right now. All this bully beef is churning up my guts, or perhaps it is the sights I am seeing. Oceans of men running towards their death, dropping like helpless flies. I must concentrate on something else. Write home, send good news.

I will close my eyes and dream of Hélène, but then I get

myself het up, wondering whether I will ever see her again. I dream of her long, dark hair, so long she must be able to sit on it. It flows down her back like melting chocolate. Chocolate. I have eaten my ration of chocolate. It was only a small slab. Food. I dream of all sorts of food, even horse meat. The French eat frogs too, so I'm told. I haven't tried them, but I will. Darn it, yes, I will. I recite all the meals I will eat when I am shot of here. Getting shot, no, I won't dwell on that. I have been living off cold beans directly out of cans, it seems for days, but I have lost count of time. When we get given beans, beans and then more beans, it means there is a shortage of meat or the catering corps cannot reach us. Where are we? How many trenches have we crossed? The fact is I am so hungry and undernourished, if they served it, right now, I'd wolf down a plate piled high with horse meat.

*Dear Mum and Dad,*

*How are you? Do you both still stroll up to Manze's for a pint of eels? I wonder what you are doing right now while I am crouched in this bloomin' trench listening to the intermittent outbursts of gunfire, fearing that the Boche will hit us again with gas?*

*Oh, dear Mum, how can I describe all that I am seeing here? The French countryside is very pretty. Lots of greenery and tall poplar trees and many villages with churches with spires and bells that don't ring because we are at war. Because it is summer, there are many roses in bloom. They climb the walls of the old buildings and bring colour and cheeriness to our days, which are not all bad. Yellow roses, red roses. A golden rose. The food is good when you can get it. I am not referring to the army grub which makes me dream of Manze's pie and your home cooking. But in the little cafés and bistros, whenever we are back from the line and in the villages with the French people, most of whom are friendly and seem glad to have us around, helping them fight Jerry. Yes, when we are with them, we get served good grub.*

*Did I tell you I met a girl? Such a girl, such a beauty. Her name is Hélène. She has hair as dark as chocolate, long and wavy, like embroidery thread. Mostly she wears it coiled up on her head in what she calls a "chignon". Her eyes are sea-blue and she is as pretty as any lass I have ever seen in London. Her lips are tinged with the pink of newly ripe strawberries. I hope one day you will meet her. Perhaps we will all travel over here together when the war is over and I can introduce you to her? I'd like that. We can have a meal all of us at her folks' café, which is called the Golden Rose. I told her they must have named the place after her.*

*Well, I'll sign off now. Better try and get some sleep.*

*Let's hope we will be together again soon.*

*Your son,*

*Dennis*

Sleep! When night falls in this infernal place, the blackness is like a cloak of death, not a darkness that encourages slumber. We crouch, we wait, we try to grab a few winks of shut-eye. When I close my eyes, I pray that no rat will come near me. Then the firing starts, lighting up the sky with its metallic explosions and that is our repose over. By the time dawn arrives, the sunbursts hurt my eyes.

*

Captain Armstrong's whistle. It is. I picked it up and slipped it into my tattered pocket when I literally stumbled over the severed body parts of what remained of my commanding officer. The poor bugger had been blasted to bits. The whistle was pockmarked in several places by bullets. I will hand it in and hope that it is returned to his family. Curious, I fought alongside this man and I know nothing at all about his personal life. He wore a wedding ring, I remember that. He wrote with a very elegant black fountain pen and he carried a leather whisky flask in a pocket of his uniform, but it is the whistle that has proved to be sturdier than the Captain.

Who will give us our orders now? Send us over towards the next onslaught?

The sad part about all this, one of many sad parts, is that there seems to be no end to it all. If we live through tonight, in the morning we will be alive but then we have to face the same all over again. And when tomorrow is over, if I survive, there will be the day after, then next week and next month. The men on stretchers, those who have been wounded not the dead, are carried back to behind the lines to base camp and no matter their pain, if they are conscious, they are happy, often laughing hysterically. They are getting out. They are going home. Whereas we who are fit must knuckle down and stay in these filthy stinking trenches and fight on. My tattered uniform reeks of blood from the corpses of dead men. My socks are soaking wet and I have holes in my boots.

*

We crossed an area of marshland today, our legs sinking into mud, until eventually, shattered, we threw ourselves down into what we thought or had been told was an enemy front-line trench, panting, breathless from running and fear. There we found that some of our own men were already there, wounded or dead. It was a ghastly spectacle and I am ashamed to say that this time I did throw up at the sight of those bodies. One bloke, dead and gone, head misshapen, mouth wide open, all his Hampsteads were missing. That's Ginger's lingo. Hampstead Heath: teeth. "Poor sod has lost his teeth," I cried, weeping and heaving. It was ludicrous of me not to be saying "poor sod has lost his life". I saw all the teeth a bit later, spilled and scattered all about him on the filthy ground like a broken necklace of pearls.

Where is Ginger? I hope he hasn't lost his Hampsteads. I hope he's still alive. Why haven't I seen him?

"Ginger! Ginger!" I yelled.

"Keep your voice down, mate," some bloke called back to me. "You trying to get us all killed?"

\*

It's raining. Rain falling into the trenches and soaking us. We are waist-deep in water and mud and there's no getting out. I found a discarded groundsheet and have been using it to try and keep out of the downpour but it has been shot so badly and there are so many holes in it that the rain leaks through it. If a gun doesn't blast us to bits, we'll die of the cold and damp on our lungs. I have named this confluence of trenches Hell's Corner.

But you know what? Hell's Corner has just become my Heaven because we have received word that we are being pulled back. We are GETTING OUT.

\*

I am at base camp. We have been relieved at the Front and given two weeks' leave. I cannot believe my good fortune. TWO WEEKS' leave. I am still alive and am being liberated, albeit for a short respite. We do not have permission to leave France or even to travel any great distance from the war zone but we are to be moved out of the line of fighting and installed further back. Somewhere close to our original billets in small towns and villages in the surrounding areas. A brief refuge, brief respite. Time to clean ourselves up, quiet our thoughts and be fed as well as possible with the provisions that are available.

And I will see Hélène. No matter where I am billeted, I will find my way to her.

*

The march back from the camp took a while. Lifting our own feet, one foot in front of the other, was a strain. One bloke just behind me collapsed with exhaustion under the weight of his pack. I and a couple of the other lads hauled him back onto his feet but his legs wouldn't straighten and we were obliged to drag and stagger with him along the road. None of us had the strength to carry him. The distance to the first village seemed to lengthen as we proceeded, not shorten. I could see a church spire and wanted to keep my sight on that, but I was so tired that if I did not concentrate on the physical business of putting one boot in front of the other, I began to get dizzy. I have never been so thankful to reach my destination. Even those who were not staying with us, paused for a rest and to drink water from the communal pump. Crowds of tired, filthy soldiers slurping at the water. How sweet that silvery liquid tasted. How happy we all were.

We were the fortunate ones. This time around, we were the fortunate ones.

I sloshed and sluiced myself with the pump water, soaking my clothes, making a right old mess in my eagerness to get the blood and muck out of my hair and off my skin.

While I was scrubbing myself, Ginger came up behind me and slapped me on the back. "How are you, mate?" We hugged like brothers. He looked a sight.

I chatted to a bloke called Terry Blume. He is a fusilier and was recounting to me how he had spent the last couple of weeks loading eighteen-pound shells onto the field guns. He said he had almost lost his hearing from being so close to the deafening explosions. Shells bursting all the time. Boom! Boom! Boom!

I was thankful I could hear the birds singing and see the life in the trees and plants, the blossoms, roses of Picardy, so brilliantly or delicately coloured, the slow-paced rhythm of ordinary farming people trying to go about their lives as best they can under appalling circumstances, nightingales singing after dark; all these details seemed like miracles after our days and nights at the mercy of shell fire while buried beneath mud, churned-up earth and foul-smelling water. It was hard to take it all in. Life. Real life. *This* was the real thing, not where we had come from.

*

We are on leave. It is hard to credit it. Leave. A short breather.

Ginger and myself and a couple of dozen others from our regiment are now billeted in yet another farmer's barn about five miles west of Bray. It's spacious and reasonably comfortable, pongs a bit of cows and their dung but it is dry and agreeably cool and this night, after all I've seen, it felt like a palace as I lay back against the straw playing tunes on my whistle. Tomorrow, I will walk to the Golden Rose for a bite to eat. I don't care how far from here it is and as long as I don't have to cross the war zone, I'll make it there and I'll be back for when they need me.

*

Heat bouncing off the walls in the villages as I stride through. Dogs lying out in the full sun. The heat is intense, and I am alive. I wave vigorously to everyone who shouts at me, "*Bonjour Tommy.*"

"*Bonjour Frenchie*, I'm alive," I yell in response.

I passed a handwritten primitively concocted sign someone had rigged up on the side of a stone house down a dusty village track. It read: "This way Leicester Square." Beneath this message was a black arrow, pointing west. I burst into grateful song.

*Singing songs of Piccadilly,*
*Strand and Leicester Square,*
*Till Paddy got excited,*
*Then he shouted to them there:*
*It's a long way to Tipperary,*
*It's a long way to go.*

*Goodbye, Piccadilly,*
*Farewell, Leicester Square…*

When I arrived at the Golden Rose, it was the middle of the day. I was tired, famished and the door was locked. I knocked and called but there was no reply. Not a soul about and no notice to say where everyone was. The family was probably up at their house eating their lunch. I decided against disturbing their mealtime, wandered down to the river and sat watching the ducks. I realized that my longing for, my desire to see Hélène had been so intense it had not been logical. It had not occurred to me that there would be no one about until later. I sat throwing small pebbles into the water, trying to make them spin, deciding what to do next. I couldn't sit there till evening. Or could I? I had walked many miles that morning and I was starving, so I decided to continue along the road into Bray and find myself some lunch, but I hadn't gone more than half a mile when I spotted Hélène walking towards me. I waved and yelled and began to run. "Hélène!"

She was slowed down by the weight of her full shopping bags. I ran so fast I almost ran into her. She was beaming at me as I approached.

"Let me take those," I trilled, grabbing her load.

"You're alive. Oh, Dennis, you're alive. We have been hearing terrible stories…"

We strolled back towards the bistro side by side, but as we approached the stone wall that flanks their roadside orchards she drew to a halt.

"It's better you don't accompany me," she said.

"Why? Don't your parents approve of me?" I hoped with all my heart this wasn't the case. I picked an apple from one of the overhanging branches and bit into it. It was too young; green and sharp.

"No, it's not that. They are all waiting for lunch. I have the provisions from the market and I mustn't dally," she laughed as I screwed up my face. "Will you come to tea this afternoon? Maman said that if you came back from the war," she stopped, understanding the impact of "if". "Maman said when you come back, if you came to see us again, she wants to talk to you."

"Let me carry the bags to the door for you."

She shook her head. "I'll see you later." And off she went, determined but laden.

How about that. I have been invited to tea with Hélène and her mother this afternoon.

*

Hélène's house is set back behind the bistro at the far end of a yard, where a flock of geese, about a dozen chickens, a few guinea fowl and a young grey donkey were enjoying residence. In the stable abutting the left side of the house, a strong brown mare peered out from her box. As I approached she plodded forward and stuck out her head, ears pricked up, watching my arrival with thoughtful eyes. Might she recognize the sound of my scruffy boots, my tread on the stones or perhaps she pops her head out to greet all passers-by? I was a bit too early for my tea appointment so I was glad to have a reason not to ring the bell too soon and look overly keen.

"Hello, girl," I called as I turned by the ancient water pump and approached the mare. She neighed and shook her head, which ruffled her mane.

"If I were back home in London, I'd bring you an apple." I was stroking her muzzle. It was as soft as my mother's knitting wool. I realized then that promising her an apple was ridiculous because Hélène's family have orchards behind the house so this mare probably eats more apples than any horse can stomach.

"No, you don't want an apple," I apologized, "they are very sour. But I tell you what, next time I'm passing and I have a minute to spare, I'll sing you a ditty," and I bid her good afternoon.

*

Hélène opened the door a little shyly and showed me through into their "best room". *Le salon du Dimanche*. Usually used only on Sundays, she explained, but since war broke out, it had become an area for the women to work in. My sweetheart, who had put on a very elegant frock and dressed her hair in a looser style, disappeared to fetch the tea. Although it was early afternoon, the oil lamp was lit. A trio of dainty china cups and saucers had been laid out on a white lace tablecloth. The room smelt slightly musty as though it had been closed up for a long spell. Madame Gaston, Hélène's mother, a rather refined lady in a pretty green dress edged with lace around the neck, was seated by the lamp, worrying at a white handkerchief grasped between her fingers. Her lips were moving and I thought she might be silently praying. The softly burning light ironed out the lines on her face creating a delicate, younger complexion. She looked rather serene.

"Ah, Monsieur or perhaps I should address you as Private Stoneham," she said in perfect but heavily accented English. "*Asseyez-vous*. Please sit down." She stretched out her arm and I panicked, unsure whether she wanted to shake my hand or was pointing to a chair.

I was jittery with nerves. Foolish. Here I was in France to fight a war. I had survived so far, was still alive, in possession of all my limbs, and now quaking in my boots at taking tea with a not-so elderly woman with poor eyesight. I saw at close range how pretty she once must have been. It runs in the family.

"Please call me Dennis," I spluttered, almost choking, because I suddenly had a bit of a frog in my throat.

"Very well then, Dennis. You play the piano with great aplomb, if I may say."

"Thank you, Madame. Music is where my heart is."

"Were you attending a *conservatoire* in England, Dennis, when the war broke out?"

"Sorry, what's that?"

"Were you studying at an academy of music?"

"Lord, no. I've never had a lesson in me life. I've taught myself. Piano, banjo, ukulele. I can't even read music. Well, a little bit, I can. I was trying to get to grips with it back home before I was sent over here. I wish I had them with me now: my ukulele and my banjo. Musical instruments are companions to me. Friends. I've played the string instruments since I was a kid but my dad bought me the piano last year so I've only been playing the keys for about eighteen months. It cuts me up something proper to have left them all behind. I would like to play for you."

"Only eighteen months and no training? It is hard to believe. Clearly, you have a natural aptitude."

"Cheers, thanks. Well, as I say, self-taught, intuitive rather than schooled. I didn't have any teachers but I have always wanted to go into the musical hall, so…"

I couldn't stop talking, fifteen to the dozen, just like at the lake with Hélène.

"Of course, I never really thought I would or could, but now I say to myself: Dennis, when this war is over, if you get out of this alive… Well, Madame, I intend to aim for what I dream of, to fulfil those dreams, to make them come true. And no one will stop me. I want to sing and play, entertain and go on the stage." I was like a steam train, chuntering on and on.

"Good gracious."

I think I shocked her.

Hélène arrived with a tray. On it was a teapot that matched the cups and a strainer. I was mighty delighted to see her, feeling embarrassed that I had not known what a *conservatoire* was and that I am just a self-taught musician and perhaps the music hall is not Madame's idea of real performance. I had been so anxious to make a good impression.

"*Chérie*, this young man, Dennis, has never had a music lesson in his life."

Hélène was pouring the tea. "Did I tell you, Dennis, that Maman was a piano teacher?"

I shook my head and accepted the proffered cup. It danced and bounced on its saucer because I was shaking like a leaf. I placed the cup quickly onto the lace tablecloth, knowing that I wouldn't dare to pick it up again.

"Here in Picardy, we Picards have our own instrument. It is a version of the bagpipes and we call it *un pipasso*," said Hélène, encouraging the conversation along while her mother grappled, fingers searching, for the milk and waved her hand agitatedly when Hélène tried to pass the jug to her.

"Never heard of it!" I laughed. Everything Hélène says makes me laugh not necessarily because it is funny but because I am so full of happiness when I am near her that I fear I might burst with it, and laughing seems to help me contain it.

"When we have finished our tea, Hélène, why don't we walk up to the bistro and open up the piano?"

And that was what we did.

Inside the empty restaurant, Madame Gaston sat down at the stool, guided by her glorious daughter, and ran her fingers up and down the black-and-white notes as though she was saying hello to them. "*Bonjour*, it's me, the lady in green. I'm back. Let's make some music together."

Somehow, her diminishing sight seemed to enhance her relationship with the instrument she clearly knew so well. And then she began to play. Hélène and I were seated on chairs next to one another at one of the dining tables behind her mother who, I think, had forgotten we existed. She was lost to us, transporting herself into another world. I didn't recognize the piece she was playing. The style of music was more serious than I am used to. Classical, I suppose you would call it, but I liked it and I did not feel excluded by it.

I was fighting the impulse to brush my fingers across Hélène's hands resting in her lap.

When Madame had finished, she remained motionless with her hands limp on the keyboard, and she waited. We were silent until she swung her body towards us, almost like a girl. She was radiant, had lost fifteen years.

"*Clair de Lune.* It is the third movement from the *Suite bergamasque* by Claude Debussy. He lives in Paris. Do you know his work, Dennis?"

I shook my head.

"I will teach this movement to you. I have no idea how much free time they will be allocating you while you are here in the army, but it would give me enormous pleasure to work a little with you and it will encourage me to play again, to rediscover the joy music gives me. As it does to you."

I was dumbfounded. For two reasons. Firstly, I would have the use of their piano and I would be playing with someone who had far greater skills than my own…

"What do you say, Dennis?"

I threw a look to Hélène, who was smiling radiantly. The proposition seemed to please her as well. And that was the second reason; I would be close to Hélène.

"I am honoured. Thank you. I have been given two weeks' leave beginning today, so…"

"Then we will commence tomorrow morning at ten, does that suit you?"

"It certainly does." And before I knew what I was doing, I whisked up a couple of spoons from the table, laid and prepared for the evening's dinner service, and slapping the spoons together and against my knees, I rattled out a little tune, some silly nonsense I made up there and then. Almost like a jig of happiness. Both my companions laughed.

I rose to go and Hélène accompanied me to the door.

"Dennis," called Hélène's mother, as I reached for the handle. "We have a bicycle. It belongs to my son. You may have the use of it for getting yourself about, if you wish. It'll save all that walking."

I could hardly believe what I was hearing. "That's exceedingly generous of you."

"Hélène, why don't you take Dennis round to the sheds and show him where it is, there's a good girl. And hurry back, Hélène, please."

"Mercy, mercy, Madame," I nodded.

"*Merci* not mercy," corrected Hélène.

"In return, you can play for our diners of an evening, what do you say to that?"

I was grinning like a dolt, picturing Ginger and my mates and their eyes green with envy.

"Maman, you make a gesture to someone or you don't. You cannot create conditions to your kindness," cried Hélène. It was the first time I had seen any show of displeasure from her. Up to this point, I had known only a docile creature and I rather liked the spirited girl on display beside me. Even more so, because her passion was in defence of me, Dennis.

"I like to play," I winked. "It will be a pleasure for me and I can practise in the evenings what I have been taught during the morning. Sounds good. See you tomorrow, Madame."

*

Hélène and I walked to the shed in silence. She was a step or two ahead of me, striding forward, leading the way. I could hear my boots crunching on the stone track as I trailed her, admiring her figure, watching her long hair bouncing against her back when, suddenly, she swung round and I almost bumped into her.

"She is doing this on purpose," she cried.

"Doing what?"

"Those nosy farmers' wives saw us sitting by the river, Dennis, and they tittle-tattled to Maman and Grandma. Maman knows too well that if she forbids me to be alone with you again, I will disobey her and we will meet clandestinely. So, she needs to steal all your attention, then there will be no possibility for us to sneak away and spend time in one another's company. She is too cunning."

There was a frown furrowing her forehead. I wanted to stroke it to smoothness. My heart was brimming over at the knowledge that Hélène cared to be alone with me and that she could be upset at the prospect that someone, even her own mother, should "steal" our precious time together. I lifted my hand and touched her cheek. I so longed to take her in my arms and kiss her.

III

"I love you," I breathed, words barely spoken, out before I knew it. She gazed with her big eyes at me, full of surprise and questions, and then to my amazement she leaned towards me, pecked me softly on the cheek, swung on her heels and dragged the shed door open as though she intended to wrench it from its hinges.

"*Voilà*, Pierre's bicycle, Dennis. We will see you tomorrow. The bistro is not open this evening." And with that she had sped away and I was left alone staring at my new transport. I had not even known Hélène had a brother until Madame Gaston mentioned him. There is so much to learn about the girl I love.

# HÉLÈNE

I have turned the key in the lock so that no busybody can barge in without knocking. Papa is sleeping in my parents' room. I can hear his snores from along the corridor. Maman and Grandma are on the top floor, closed in with the cottons and bobbins. Their laughter rings out even to here. It is so long since they have hidden themselves away sharing their confidences that I wonder what is going on. Are they plotting against me, against Dennis and me? Is Grandma advising Maman on ingenious ways to keep me from being alone with Dennis? Neither of them have mentioned our afternoon by the river but I know for sure that Madame Cheron and Madame Thibaud told tales. It is obvious.

I would like to suggest to Dennis that we run away together but it is impossible when there is a war on. We cannot go anywhere and he would almost certainly be arrested. If Pierre was here, I could ask his advice, enlist his help, but there is nobody for me to talk to, except Dennis and that would be awkward.

He said he loves me, but so softly were his sentiments spoken that I do not think he intended me to hear him.

Yet, he must have been talking to me. His feelings cannot be for another, can they? I am so inexperienced in all these matters. It is very frustrating.

Perhaps I should be brave and say outright to Maman and Grandma that I love Dennis and want to be with him and then see what they advise. If they do not approve of him, then surely they would not encourage his presence at the bistro.

I have decided that grown-up women are rather dissembling. As Madame Thibaud said, they never tell their secrets to men and they plot together like covens of witches.

Will I become like them when I am older? Did Maman and Grandma plot to get my father to marry into this family? Is Maman being kind inviting Dennis to play the piano with her and to spend his evenings here with us or does she have an ulterior, wicked motive?

I am sure I have no answers to my questions. Love is a complex affair.

Do I *love* Dennis? If loving him means I feel joyous in his company, that I long for him to be close to me, I dream about him kissing me, then yes, yes, I do believe I love him.

# DENNIS

This morning I had my first piano lesson. It was fascinating and great fun. Madame Gaston is a kind if rather formal lady. She is a fine teacher and patient with me, although I didn't ask too many questions and I managed to keep quiet and not rabbit on, as I had done yesterday. She says that she does not wish to influence my style of playing, which, she says, is my very own. She wishes only to assist me with the theory of music and to make sure I know all twelve sets of scales and to explain to me the complexity of chord structures so that I can compose with a wider understanding of the possibilities of music. She said that I have a natural ear for popular music and that if I listen carefully to any style at all, I will be able to interpret it to my own way of playing and my own compositions. This elated me. Madame Gaston gives me confidence. After our lesson was over, she played another classical piece. She wanted to acquaint me with the music she enjoys. Again, this was far more serious than my own repertoire. And then she invited me up to the house to have lunch with her and the rest of the family. As we were about to close up the restaurant, she laid her hand on my arm, drawing me back an instant.

"One question, please, Dennis, if I may?"

"Of course, what is it?" I grew nervous, thinking she was going to quiz me about my feelings for Hélène.

"How does it go for you, Dennis?" she asked with an intensity that took me by surprise. She must have registered my confusion because she added, "Your life fighting in the trenches?"

I went cold. I did not want to discuss the subject. Being with the Gastons is my way of blotting the haunting images out, keeping the horrors at bay, but I also did not feel able to dismiss this woman after her kindnesses towards me.

"I try to keep my spirits up," I said, "playing tunes, thinking about my home and those I love."

"Do you have nightmares?"

"It's not always easy to sleep," I conceded, remembering the nights of insomnia, the awakening dawns that stung my exhausted eyes.

"As you know, I have a son out there somewhere, Dennis. I fear it must be the same for Pierre," she said. "I fear he lies awake at night, carrying the war in his every thought. But we wait to receive his next letter so I don't know how he is coping with the dangers and I am growing so afraid."

What could I say, after all that I have witnessed? Two months ago, I would have offered a winning smile and made light of her concerns but try as I did, I simply could not muster up platitudes, empty reassurances. The French Army was losing as many men as we were.

"I hope you will receive a letter soon," I murmured.

"Of course. Foolish of me. We each must find a way to cope. Come, Dennis, the others will be getting hungry."

I had let her down. Such a generous lady, who I had so wanted to please. But how could I pretend that all is well when it is not?

*

There are five of them living in that huge old house. The grandparents are Monsieur and Madame Dumont and then there is Hélène along with her parents. We ate in their kitchen, crammed with copper plates of every shape and size, each piled high with vegetables still covered in earth. The meal had been laid out on a square, rough-hewn wooden table. Pine wood. The carpentry was basic. I wanted to tell them that Dad could have styled them a very elegant oak table to fit perfectly into that space, and who knows perhaps one day he will. Or perhaps when I am more skilled, I will fashion it myself.

There were pots and kettles and cooking utensils, dried herbs and flowers hanging from the wooden beams that crossed the ceiling and farming implements hanging from every wall. It was a country space entirely occupied and it smelt of warm cooking juices and spices, not that I could decipher the scent of one herb from a spice. The meal was simple: leek tart served with big baked potatoes followed by stewed apples from the garden filled with sugar and dried raisins. Delicious. Hélène's grandmother offered her apologies, saying that in better times, the portions would have been more generous, that in better times the apples would have been left on the trees another five weeks to ripen, to grow fatter and sweeter. But in these days, everybody was obliged to harvest while they were able before the crops were stolen.

"The meal sufficed for me," I told them. "Delicious, mercy."

"*Merci*," grinned Hélène.

I hadn't met the old-timer before, Monsieur Dumont. What a decent, warm-hearted chap he is, insisting I drink a mug of cider with him. He had come in from working in the fields and was at the table in his shirtsleeves and brown hat. His hands were the texture of walnut shells, knobbly and calloused with the soft-chestnut hue of dried earth. His fingernails were ridged and encrusted with black from digging. His hands trembled as he tore at the baguette bread. It was as though he were ripping up a sheet. The family dog who had spent the morning out on the land with the muscular old man, followed Monsieur Dumont to the table and then settled quietly at his master's socked feet. Monsieur Dumont had left his boots outside the back door because they were coated in mud.

During the meal, I became aware that my legs were going

numb. Raynar, I think that is the dog's name, had vacated his original position and had resettled himself, stretched full length across my lower calves and ankles, and he was heavy. He's almost the size of their donkey.

The grandparents don't speak any English so Hélène and her mum did the translating. Hélène's dad, who seems friendly but did not say too much, ate his food quickly and then retired for a nap. I think he was a bit confused as to what I was doing there having lunch with them, though he seemed delighted at the idea that I'd be the resident entertainment at the bistro.

Monsieur Dumont said that if I have any energy left after my evening piano playing and my morning lessons, he could do with some strong arms out in the fields. I said I'd lend a hand as long as I'm here. It might be wartime, he reminded us, but the harvests still need to be brought in.

Feeling uncomfortable when silence descended upon the room and there was nothing but the repetitive sound of jaws chewing, I thanked the family for their kindnesses towards me and for the loan of Pierre's bicycle and said that I would bring it straight back again if their son returned and needed it. My innocent yet careless remark caused visible upset and I wished I had kept quiet.

"No one has heard from Pierre in over a year," returned Hélène's dad. His words needed to be translated so involved Hélène repeating them.

Madame Gaston emphasized to me how important it was to write to my parents at least once a week. I assured her I was doing just that.

"I have nightmares that my Pierre will never return," she whispered.

I could have bitten off my tongue.

*

After lunch, I needed to stretch my legs, get some life back into them. I went out into the courtyard and the dog romped along after me. Monsieur Dumont passed me and tipped his hat. As he climbed up onto his wagon, he whistled to Raynar. The dog ignored his boss and remained stubbornly at my shins, tongue hanging out, panting contentedly, refusing to obey the farmer.

"Go on, off you go," I commanded. The animal took no notice. I was on my way to park the bicycle in the shed for the afternoon. Raynar followed.

The old farmer seated patiently in his wagon whistled and then called me over. He signalled to me to jump up and accompany him to the fields. I dithered like a fool, having secretly counted on snatching a couple of precious hours with Hélène, who was presently washing up. My plan had been to offer to scrub and dry the pots and plates in the kitchen and afterwards suggest a sunny afternoon stroll by the river, just the two of us. Hélène's grandmother along with Madame Gaston had disappeared off somewhere; her dad was sleeping;

here was the perfect opportunity for me to be alone with my girl for a couple of hours, but the old fellow wouldn't take no for an answer. So the dog, along with this disappointed lovesick soldier, jumped aboard and set off for the potato fields in the four-wheeler. Old Dumont passed me the whip and then handed the reins to me as well. I had never driven a horse-led dray before, but I managed and delivered us safely to the fields in the sunshine. From out here, in this flat windy spot, I heard that distant boom, the rattle of guns going off. My mind was drawn to all those poor blokes struggling with the the filth and the fear.

I had been reminded, lest I should forget.

Dumont had been digging all morning. Hillocks and hillocks of potatoes were his prize, spread out across a great expanse of field, and I spent the entire afternoon sacking them up and loading them onto the transport. By the time I returned with him the light was beginning to fade, my back was killing me and I still had the prospect of three or four hours of piano-playing ahead of me for the evening diners. I was filthy and completely exhausted. It didn't matter. Dumont insisted we drink another cider together. To wash down the dirt, he winked. After the refreshment, I felt better than I had in months. I felt at peace, embraced by the company of good people, a family unit tending their lives. Here, for a short time, I could set aside the nightmares in my head, and whatever lay ahead for me when I returned to the trenches. Old man Dumont lent me a pail from the kitchen and I spruced myself up outside at the ancient pump.

The dog sat at my side as though he'd been with me all his life.

"You've taken a bit of a fancy to me, haven't you, mate? Shadow of Dennis, that's who you are." And blow me, but the dog answered to the nickname.

I sang a few notes to the mare who had popped out her head to say hello. "Are you getting jealous of my pal here?"

*"If you were the only girl in the world…"*

*I could live this life*, I was thinking, the two animals gazing at me as though I was their best pal. *I'll marry Hélène, toil the land, do a little carpentry, sell my furniture to earn us a living, have kids – not too many – run our own café where we can offer evenings of musical entertainment…* There was no need to remind myself that in less than two weeks, I'd be back at the Front.

*

Once I was clean, Hélène and her dad fed me some dinner in the bistro kitchen and then sent me to the piano. Hélène barely caught my eye and I was concerned that I might have upset her. Surely she had not heard me when I breathed the words, "I love you," and if she had, had they angered her?

Regulars were arriving. Always they stopped by the

piano to shake my hand. *"Bonsoir, monsieur,"* they would say to me. I felt a part of the scene, integral to the party. The French hereabouts really seem to enjoy my musical-hall ditties and the room was beginning to fill up, was getting smoky and lively when Ginger, Charley, Jackson and a few other soldiers, mates of mine, came strolling in. I was tinkling at the keys, running my fingers up and down the black and whites, deciding what to play next when Ginger came up behind me and slapped me on the back. "I might have guessed I'd find you here. We were beginning to wonder if you'd gone AWOL."

I froze. I hoped he was joking.

Absent Without Leave gets you court-martialled and then follows the firing squad.

"I might not be the bravest, mate, but I won't be shirking my duty." I was trying to make light of it.

At that instant, Hélène appeared from the kitchen with a tray laden with plates of steaming food. Ginger forgot me and skidded across to her, "Let me take that", and unlike my catastrophic attempt when I sent the crockery spinning to the floor, he handled it with perfect grace, serving each table as though born to be a waiter. In fact, for the next hour or so he assisted her with the service. She took the orders and he lugged the trays, empty and full, to and from the kitchen. They seemed very companionable, perfectly at ease with one another, laughing as they worked, standing close as they discussed orders and my heart lurched. I thought Ginger might be a little put out by my various arrangements with the Gaston family when he found out about them, but it was *me* who was feeling a bit put out and, if I am honest, more than a little jealous.

*At this rate, the Gastons will have the entire British Army working their estate*, I was thinking as I fed out a few tunes and sang along to them. He hasn't said as much but Ginger does have his eye on Hélène and clearly intends to give me a run for my money. My mind was racing as I performed, going back over my moments with Hélène. Did I have any certainty that she shared my feelings?

\*

When the doors were closed and only Hélène remained clearing up in the bistro, adamantly refusing all offers of assistance from either Ginger or myself, Ginger assumed I would be walking back with him and the other lads.

"I'll catch up with you later," I said, trying to shrug off the fact that I had the bike. I could have left it in the shed and walked with my mates but then I would have had to be up at the crack of dawn to retrace my footsteps for my piano lesson.

"What are you waiting about for, hoping for another glimpse of the girl?" He was joking but at the same time, he wasn't.

"Let the lad alone. If he wants to hang about, that's his

affair. We have a long walk. Let's get on the road." I don't know if Charley was just tired or attempting to intervene on my behalf but it had the desired effect. Jackson and Terry Blume, the fusilier, also nagged at Ginger to get going. So, eventually, Ginger sloped off with the others. I hung back a few minutes until they were well on their way and then I ran to the shed and wheeled out the bike.

My two-wheeled steed and I whizzed along the dark country lanes. I took the longer route back to my billet, my hay barn, following the lakes and donkey trails, so that I could enjoy the stars and avoid passing the other chaps on their hike home. As I flew along, I judged myself to be the luckiest man on French soil.

Blessed, is what I am. At least, I hope I am.

# HÉLÈNE

The days seem to have passed so fast. Too, too quickly. Dennis shared his last piano class with Maman this morning and entertained us in the bistro for the last time this evening. The last time that is until he returns, which I pray will be very soon.

After we closed the restaurant before Papa went off to bed, he gave Dennis a hearty handshake for all the support he has given us. "There's always a job for you here, should you want one," he grinned. I translated, of course. "Keep yourself safe, lad, and stay in touch."

Our covers have almost doubled over the past two weeks and Papa is convinced that offering music makes all the difference. "That boy and his London songs have cheered us Picards up no end," he declared while we were preparing the entrées in the kitchen this evening, "and I believe our Golden Rose has given some of those soldiers a few happy memories to take back to their various countries with them. When they talk of the war, they will talk of us."

"Don't make it all sound so final, Papa," I begged him as he chopped at onions, while tears streamed down his cheeks and he consoled himself with a large glass of white wine. "This horrid war is not over yet, alas. There will be plenty more soldiers passing through and Dennis will be back as soon as he is given leave again."

"Let's hope so, girl," was my father's rather unnerving response. Or am I just being ultra-sensitive?

At the end of the evening, I accompanied Dennis to the beginning of the lane. Earlier, he had deposited Pierre's bike in the shed as he was intending to walk back to his billet tonight. I felt sick with sadness. We strolled in silence, keeping step, and then stood, bodies facing one another, our heads bowed, both of us. He took my hand.

"I learnt a French sentence," he whispered. "I would like to say it to you. May I?"

"Of course."

"Jer tem."

I was confused, searching for meaning. Until he repeated it, doing what he always does when he is struggling to be understood, speaking louder and more emphatically. "JER TEM, Hélène. I LOVE YOU, silly."

I burst out laughing into the darkness, breaking open with happiness, releasing my pent-up sadness and because he is the sweetest, loveliest person in the world. "*Je t'aime*," I corrected.

"Do you? Do you, Hélène, love me because if you do… oh, this war. This bleedin' war. Do you love me? I need to hear it, Hélène, even if I shouldn't ask and it is not correct behaviour."

"*Je t'aime*, Dennis."

"Do you mean it? I mean you are not just saying so because I am going back to the trenches to face whatever I must…"

"Stop." I put my hand on his arm.

"Can I kiss you? Just once. What will your dad say? Can they see us out of their window? Can I kiss you? Oh, come here." He pulled me into his arms, buried his face, his lips in the crook of my neck and shoulder and held me so tight I thought I would suffocate. "Jer tem. Jer tem. Jer tem," he mumbled.

I felt a longing shoot through me, a desire I have never known before. I wanted him to hold me tighter still, to touch me and never let me go. He lifted his face from my neck and brushed his stubbled cheek against mine. It was rough and scratched my skin, but the discomfort excited me, sent a thrill up from my lower body. Then he pressed his lips against mine. He kissed me so hard, pushing into me, I lost my footing. I stumbled backwards. He grabbed me, pulled me back to my full height, held me again. He was breathing so hard, so fast, I grew a little afraid and tried to ease myself from his grip. "You're frightening me," I muttered into his flesh.

Suddenly, he went still as though calming himself and

then released me, keeping his head bowed, not looking at me. "Don't be angry."

I was taken aback, puzzled by this. "I'm not angry."

"I better go. I didn't mean to take advantage, you know that, don't you? I just wanted to kiss you, to hold you. I love you so much it torments me."

And then he lifted his head and those green tortured eyes bored into me. "I'd never hurt you, you know that, don't you? I love you. Jer tem."

"I know you do, Dennis. *Moi aussi*. I love you too."

"I'll see you before long. Wait for me, Hélène. Please." And with that he leaned forward, kissed my mouth softly, gazed once more into my face, turned and headed away without looking back.

*

Alone in my room, I could not sleep. I was charged up, like a racehorse. I wanted to run back over everything, relive every moment we have spent together over these past few weeks. Last Sunday, when he drove Maman and me to church in the horse and dray. It was a golden day. Maman sat beside him and I just behind him, gazing at his hair, his profile as he leaned over to speak to Maman, to sing to her, charming her, making her laugh, describing to her the landscape as we drove through it.

His awkwardness in the Catholic church. A service he did not comprehend. During the Mass, the Holy Communion

129

ritual. The Latin. Still, he escorted Maman up the aisle to the altar for the partaking of the wafer and wine. He showed such respect, neatly attired in his uniform. He who is usually so full of verve, so funny, showed a serious, more pensive side to his nature. Even Maman remarked upon it.

"He is a unique and gifted young man, Hélène," she said later. "But we cannot forget that these are exceptional times, forced circumstances. When this war is over he will be returning to his life in England. He is not a country boy. He is from the city and his dreams are city dreams. He would never settle among us, Hélène. I sense that you are smitten, but you are ill-advised to set your heart on him. He is not for you, Hélène. He is only passing through."

I hated her for these words. *What do you know?* I wanted to shout at her. *You cannot* see. *Cannot see the depth of the love Dennis and I have for one another.*

# DENNIS

Going in again. It was difficult, more difficult even than I had steeled myself for. Leaving Hélène, entrenching myself again, taking up my position as a cog of the war. It took us two days to reach this position, marching north-east and I am not quite sure where I am now.

We have a new commanding officer. I think it is a temporary post for him although he is a solid military man and not a conscript. Balding Colonel Atkins, a fair bit older and stouter than Armstrong was. He keeps himself to himself and doesn't seem to know any of our names. Fine by me. I understand we are going for another major strike. The artillery will go first, wipe out the Germans, flatten the surrounding lands and then we, the infantry, will attack.

It all sounds so easy when these officers describe to us how it is going to be, but out here buried behind sacks, barbed wire and earth, it is quite a different story. Many of the blokes have taken to the rum, but I am abstaining. I want my wits about me.

The shells are coming over thick and fast now. Earth and stones are flying everywhere. When debris hits us, it cuts into our flesh. The damage hurts but is not as lethal as the bullets, of course. My greatcoat is wrapped like a blanket about me to act as a protection but it stifles me. I turn my head to and fro, looking about me, squinting all along the trench. There are a few men moving. In a long row, men are crouching. Piles of corpses surround us like furniture stacked for a house move. While we are waiting for orders, I settle back as best I can and play my whistle, play some of the songs I learned at the Golden Rose. That tune that Hélène's mother taught me. *Au Clair de la Lune*. Its simplicity is perfect for my tin whistle.

"*My candle is dead, I have no light…*"

Curious, I thought I heard someone else playing a whistle earlier, but if I did, he has packed it up now.

*

There are cornfields ahead of us in No Man's Land. It is harvesting time, but these crops are not going to be gathered. When a platoon crosses through them, bayonets at the ready, the steel glitters in the sunlight and can be seen above the blades of tall corn, field after field of corn already golden and our men are tramping paths through them. Blades of silver steel, blades of soft bending gold. Gold and silver. Life and death.

I am reminded of the late afternoon I spent rabbit hunting with old man Dumont. Such a nice bloke. We waited, crouched down in a cornfield until it was the hour for the rabbits and hares to come up from their burrows to feed. We had set the snares that morning before my piano lesson. Most were empty so we hid and waited for them to return. Two hares we trapped. I wouldn't, couldn't, shoot them. We bagged them and drove them back to the bistro. Dumont told me in our pidgin conversations that the brown hare can run at almost thirty-five miles an hour. Monsieur Gaston said he would roast them both for the family lunch and we ate them piping hot the following midday, washed down with a couple of glasses of local table wine.

Oh, how I miss that rural harmony. I could get used to it.

\*

On several occasions recently when all is quiet and we are hunched down in our trench trying to make the best of it, with the ghost of a quarter moon high in the daytime sky, I have been catching the distant strains of music. Whistling. I hear whistling. It is not in my mind. Another bloke making music somewhere in the distance?

\*

Heavy strafing tonight. Jerry has been pasting the whole area, and just to make matters worse, it's very damp in the trench. We have been told to ready ourselves to move at a moment's notice. But to go where? To another bloody trench. The frame of mind amongst the lads is low, sinking into the mud. Many seem down in the dumps. Ha! Down in the dumps, indeed. Down in the trenches is what we are.

I hear the boom of guns and then the fade of the booming guns. My throat is dry as dead leaves or I'd get out my whistle and attempt a tune.

Is there any just cause to go to war? I suppose this question makes me sound like a traitor to my country and the cause. I am not.

*

Stretcher cases are awaiting removal but no stretcher-bearers are getting through to fetch them. Men who might have been saved are breathing their last.

They have brought wagonloads of big guns right up to the Front Line and are shooting them from here. Their relentless blasts practically blow my head off and make my ears ring.

I have learnt a new expression: short daily artillery bombardments made by either side and aimed at disrupting enemy routines are known as "hates". What a horrid expression. I know the Hun is our enemy and all that, but somehow I never expected all this. Shooting with hate. I don't hate anyone. I don't even hate the enemy. They are just blokes in different trenches with different uniforms and another language.

*

At first, I thought I was imagining the other musician, another soldier playing a whistle, but I am not. We have been stuck in this same trench for several days now. There is a German battalion in an enemy trench, beyond No Man's

Land, about two hundred yards away. They are the other side of the demarcation line. There in that trench, a German, an enemy soldier is playing a whistle, probably not dissimilar to mine. How can I hate a fellow musician? I don't recognize any of his tunes, possibly because I cannot always precisely pick out the notes. It's the wind that carries them over to me. If they are German melodies, I have probably never heard them before or perhaps, like me, Jerry is composing his own arias, making them up as he goes along, to give his day some creative purpose, to help blot out the destruction.

This morning I pulled out my whistle and played a tune. Jerry was silent. I listened carefully and then about – oh, hard to give any indication of time – but some little later, he began to play. It was the opening notes of *my* tune. I followed suit and added a few more notes. He did the same and on we went until we had a little improvisation going on. It really raised my morale until out of the blue a Scotsman further along in my trench yelled out with a mighty force, "Shut up that bloody racket, soldier, or I'll see you get court-martialled for colluding with the enemy."

Colluding with the enemy! What a bloody absurdity!

I took no notice. Let them court-martial me for my music. What difference would it make? In defiance, I blew a few more notes.

"You are giving us away!" he yelled again. "It's a trick."

A trick?

"Your playing tells them where we are, where there are living soldiers. That's why Jerry plays, to lead you on, you bloody fool."

I could not believe such an innocent exchange could conceal such a mercenary intent, but no sooner had the Scot spoken, than there was a break in these "pleasantries", this solo musical interlude of mine, as a big one came whizzing over. In the subsequent explosion, two blokes up the trench from me copped it. Another had his legs blown off. I was crouched, hands on head, squashed between mud, sandbags, death and falling stones, still clutching my whistle, watching two limbs flying into the filthy, ashen, stinking space around me. A soldier, the man without legs, was screaming with pain. I could just make out his voice in between the shells and the gunshots. It was the Scot who had threatened to have me court-martialled or I think it was him.

"You all right, mate?" I yelled out. I supposed I should not have been shouting if that was alerting the enemy to our positions, to where there is life, but I couldn't ignore him, could I?

I turned this way and that. I couldn't see a living soul. Where were the other lads?

"Hang on, mate, I'm on my way."

Was I responsible for this? Had my music caused these deaths?

I let go my whistle, which I saw now was all bent and

no more use to anyone, and I twisted about and managed to lay myself flat, scrambling on my belly, dragging myself like a serpent to reach the injured soldier. Wet beneath me. God knows what mixture of fluids were there. I thought I would throw up but I had to do something, to help, to shut up his screaming. It was too late for the other pair. They were both gone.

"Come on, mate," I said, panting and exhausted when I reached him. "Can you move at all?" He didn't answer. I think he must have passed out with the pain. I turned myself around so I was facing back to where I'd come from – did it make any difference? It took all my strength and willpower and downright stubbornness, but somehow, dragging and shoving, I hauled the wounded soldier onto my back. Then, slowly, I began to snake my way back to my spot, but I had to take several rest breaks along the way because the effort was doing me in.

What are my chances of ever getting out of here?

"Hélène!" I was calling out. Will I ever see Hélène again?

I must have fallen asleep or lost consciousness. I dreamt I caught sight of Ginger riding atop of one of the new tanks that have just arrived.

"I'm getting a free ride," he called out to me. "I'm going to the Golden Rose to fetch Hélène."

Could he see me in the trench with a weight on my back?

"Ginger, give us a lift! We need a ride! Ginger, wait for us!"

Jerry was firing bullets from every direction. I, with the load on my back, tried to shuffle my way to safety. I had to save two lives now, had to get us to a communication trench.

*

I thought Ginger would cop it. As the tanks were passing our guns, a shrapnel shell exploded right behind him.

"Ginger!" I yelled, about to jump to my feet and run after him, certain he'd roll off and be a-gonna. But I couldn't move and he was fine. He was rapping on the body of the tank as though it were a door, shouting, "Will someone let me in, please? It's raining cats and dogs out here."

"Ginger! Ginger!"

*

"Lad, calm yourself down."

When I woke up or came to, I was shouting Ginger's name, just like I had been calling out to Hélène.

"It's just a bad dream, lad."

Then I understood I was still in the mud. The stench, untenable. And I was bleeding. Had I been shot? Was this a bad dream? It's all a bloody bad dream. I was separated from my comrades. Charley, Ginger, they are nowhere in sight. I hadn't seen them for days. Last time at the Golden Rose. Did we all come here together? Hélène, my golden rose. I think Ginger's sweet on Hélène. I thought he was on a tank. There are no tanks here. I must be hallucinating.

Bullets were flying again, in all directions. Clods of earth were smacking me in my face. I tried to lift myself up. Out of the line of fire. Or was that into the line of fire? There was a weight on my back. A stone weight. I was bleeding.

There is a bloke on my back. Is he dead? Where is everyone? I have to get this bloke to safety. Must save his life.

How will Hélène know how much I love her? Will someone get a message to Hélène? Ask her to marry me.

Ginger! Charley! Captain Armstrong! Where is everybody? Hélène, Hélène. I wish this rotten war was over. I have to get this bloke to safety. Must save his life. Get us out of here!

# HÉLÈNE

This morning Papa managed to buy some freshly caught eel from further upriver. He came back with two bags of them before lunch, looking pleased as punch with himself.

"It's a long time since we've tasted any of these," he said triumphantly.

I begged him to make a pie to go with it. "Please, Papa, please." It won't be the same as the dish Dennis has talked about from his home in London town, but it might remind him of his real life and it will give me such pleasure to see his face when I announce that eel is on the menu. I am praying he comes in this evening, though of course I don't know where he is; whether he is on leave, working from one of the base camps, transporting ammunitions. I hope he is not in the trenches. We haven't seen or heard of him for days, for more than two weeks. Papa said they were talking at the market this morning about the heavy fighting in the area of Estrées. Wherever Dennis is, I pray he is safe and, best of all, I so hope that he comes here tonight and tastes our eel and pie.

*

As though my prayers of earlier in the evening had been answered, as I was serving mashed turnips into a dish, the door opened and in walked Ginger. My pulse began to race and I could not stop myself from grinning. They were back. Safe. They have come to eat with us tonight. Ginger was accompanied by several others I recognized from his regiment. When he walked in the door, my heart soared because I knew it meant that Dennis was but a few steps behind him. Except that he wasn't. Five men including Ginger strolled in, in single file. They were not looking their habitually high-spirited selves. Ginger, more than any other in their team, can normally be counted on to lift the mood of the moment. He was carrying his cap in his hands, rolling it back and forth as though he were screwing up a newspaper. His eyes danced back and forth as though he were looking for someone or something. When I came out from the kitchen, he lifted his hand in a half-hearted wave. I grinned and signalled that I would be over to serve them soon.

"Two other groups first," I shouted and smiled.

His friends had settled themselves at a round table in the corner. They were all hunched in towards each other as though about to talk secrets. Where was Dennis? I think I knew then that something was up. Their mood was too grave for an evening out on the town. Ginger eyed me anxiously every time I stepped in and out of the kitchen with plates or cutlery or flagons of wine. It was surprising that he did not offer to help me.

Papa was at the stove. His receding hair plastered to his head. His big white cloth slung over his shirted shoulder. He was sweating and stirring and humming happily to himself.

"Papa," I said. "The English soldiers are here, seated at table twenty-seven. Will you give me five minutes to go and say hello to them?"

"Tell that Dennis of yours to get in here and pour his mates some drinks and let you get on with your service. And then tell him to get that piano warmed up," my father yelled in a kindly way above the cooking noises. "What does he say about the eel and pie?"

"He's not with them," I answered.

Papa stopped his stirring and swung round to face me, but I was already on my way.

"Hélène," he called after me. "I'll keep the pan heating. Go and say hello to them."

I didn't respond to him.

I returned to the restaurant but I was shaking as I took the orders from a table crammed with a French group who came in to eat with us from time to time. They were a large family from Bray-sur-Somme. The father was postmaster in the town. He and his wife had their work cut out now serving all the overseas soldiers, sending their letters to families all over the world. Many women have become involved in the postal services since the foreign soldiers arrived in the district. The pair of them often boasted about how vital their work was, and I did not doubt it. They were perfectly decent people but were always picky about their food and always insisted on knowing every ingredient in every dish including what my father had used for the sauces, which, in any case, Grandma had prepared. Since the war had begun, instead of being grateful that there was any food to be had at all for the preparation of meals, they had become even more fussy.

"You can't be too careful these days," declared the wife of the Postmaster, now the Postmistress.

"No musical entertainment tonight?" one of their party enquired. "It does make a difference. Brightens the atmosphere. Lifts the spirits."

Their orders seemed to take forever and while I waited for them while they procrastinated between rabbit stew with mashed turnips or eel and pie, I could feel the gaze of Ginger and his pals on my back. Their table was next.

Where was Dennis? Had he been wounded?

I took the last order into the kitchen and handed it to Grandma, who had just come down from the house. Papa asked me what the news was. He was shiny with heat from the steam and perspiration and he looked deeply worried. "I haven't got to them yet," I said. "Where's Maman?" I asked. Suddenly, I knew that I was going to need her.

"Lying down," Papa answered. "She's got a pain in her head behind her eyes. She thinks she strained them. Get out there and find out what the boys want to eat and where your Dennis is. Or do you want me to do it for you?"

*Your Dennis,* Papa had said.

I shook my head and left the kitchen. Something told me that when I returned to the kitchen, my life would have changed. Dennis. Suddenly I couldn't think of him as Denniz. Our private joke. Our private world.

I walked towards the boys who were gazing at me shiftily. I tried to sport a bright and cheery air in case I was over-reacting, in case my fear was playing melodramatic tricks on me.

"*Bonsoir,*" I smiled. "How are you?"

Ginger asked me did I have a couple of minutes to sit with them. He pulled out the only available chair at the table and I lowered myself into it without speaking. He bent his head and began to scramble in his little kitbag. The others said nothing, either looking at him or heads down or glancing at me but making sure not to catch my eye.

I kept my attention on Ginger's hands. Dennis's tin whistle was what he drew from his bag. It was twisted out of shape but it was surely Dennis's.

I stared at it in disbelief, feeling the tears well up into my eyes.

Ginger proffered the whistle awkwardly. "I know he would

have wanted you to have it," he said softly. "It's not much, but…"

"What happened?" I whispered staring at the whistle. My hands were trembling so violently in my lap I couldn't lift them to accept the gift.

"A shell got him. He was trying to drag one of the other blokes in the trench to safety. The soldier had had both his legs blown off and he was screaming like the devil with the pain. Dennis scrambled on his stomach to reach the geezer, to haul him on his shoulders and somehow piggyback him to somewhere where a medical aid, or God knows who, could try and help him. Another high-explosive whizzer came over the top and caught them both. Bull's eye. It finished them instantly."

I closed my eyes.

"He'll be commended for his courage. Probably be awarded a posthumous medal. We are lining up to write his praises. He was one of the best, Hélène, and he loved you with all his heart."

That was it, that final sentence went through me like a knife through butter. I felt my shoulders begin to shake. I could not thank Ginger or even look him or his comrades in the face.

Someone at table eighteen was calling for another carafe of wine. Elsewhere, diners were watching me with curiosity. People hereabouts are not strangers to bad news these days. I stumbled to my feet, struggling against tears, nodding stupidly. The whistle was resting on the table. I grabbed it and pocketed it in my pinafore, squeezing it in the palm of my hand as though it would imbue me with magical powers. At that moment my father stepped out of the kitchen. "I'll do this, love."

Ginger rose, as though shadowing me. He wrapped an arm about my shoulders, guided me through the kitchen, into the street and to our house. It had begun to rain. The chickens were flapping about, lifting their clawed feet like dancers, picking their way through the stones and mud. I nearly fell over one of them. My body seemed to be out of synch with itself.

"There was eel and pie on the menu," I stuttered stupidly.

At the door, Ginger pulled on the bell. It was a while before we heard Pappy's shuffling feet. He knew as soon as he set eyes on us.

Ginger swung me towards Pappy, who accepted me like a parcel.

"We'll just have a drink the five of us and then we'll be on our way. I'll drop by to see you tomorrow, Hélène. Try to get some sleep." He nodded to Pappy – "*merci, monsieur*" – who cradled me protectively against him, and together we watched Ginger's hunched, lanky form jog back along the rutted courtyard.

As I watched him retreat, I felt as though my life had ended.

\*

My family mourned Dennis with me for a short while and then they seemed to feel that I should get over it. Move on. Get out into the fresh air, take long walks, work harder (was that possible? I asked myself). Instead of simply waiting on tables and spending time with Papa in the overheated kitchen, they sent me off out into the fields with Pappy. They were calculating that a bit of rigorous digging would improve my circulation, rosy up my sallow cheeks, work up an appetite (not that we had much to feed on even if I had fancied it), get my heart pumping happily again. Happy heart, but mine was not. Once the war was over I would find myself a nice young French boy, Maman promised, as if they – the four adults who surround me and who claim to know best – could see into the future.

And then news came to us from the French Army that Pierre, my brother, was "Missing in Action". This usually means "killed in action". Maman was inconsolable. The local doctor had to be called in. He came by foot from Bray carrying his medicine bag to give her something to help her sleep, to steady her nerves, to calm her down. My bereavement no longer held a place in our household. Pierre's disappearance was real. He was family. Dennis had been a nice young man, but we should never forget that he had been a foreigner, merely passing through. A British soldier. We French must be kind to the soldiers, treat them with respect because they are here fighting for our rights like the rest of the Allies, until the war is over. After that, all these foreigners will decamp and France will be ours again.

But the war dragged on and on. Our two precious weeks, Dennis's and mine, were hardly an intake of breath within the war-dragon's voracious jaws.

I kept my grieving to myself. I did all I could to support my family and, without actually uttering the treacherous words, I allowed them to believe I was getting over Dennis, that I was leaving his memory behind me, sloughing my dreams.

"She's recovering," I would hear my grandma mutter to my poor mother whose sight was deteriorating rapidly now. Lost in her world of darkness and desolation, she perched up close to the lit oil lamp, groping for illumination, but she heard every sound, every whisper, and she answered the ghosts who shared her world, communed with them. She and Grandma sat together downstairs in our polished salon with its generous-sized oval dining table and lace tablecloth. Grandma was cutting the brown bits out of the gathered apples; those that were not of a sufficiently wholesome quality to be stored, but could be used for apple tart. It was the larvae of the codling moth and apple maggot that threatened to rot the fruits if not removed. The healthy apples I had packed into wooden boxes and stacked in the cellar a month or more back.

The women couldn't work outside now, sitting beside each other on the step gossiping as they had done during the summer months. Drizzle and chilly were the days as autumn crept away and left us with stark November.

Dennis, as far as the family was concerned, was the past, more or less consigned to a short summer interlude in the war's enduring story. An interlude when the piano was played, whereas the loss of Pierre was a profound tragedy. I missed Pierre too. Deeply. How I would have loved it if he and Dennis had become friends. But how many times can a heart be broken? If that beating part of me is already split asunder, do newer fractures damage it further or does it become too numb to feel any deeper, to take any more knocks? Maybe I can cut the pain out of my heart the way Grandma fillets out the maggots from the fruits?

I am ill-equipped to know the answers.

*

For as long as he stayed in the region, kind-hearted and comical Private Ginger Green paid us visits. He was a loyal customer, eating regularly at the restaurant with his chums, or sometimes he came alone, sitting in a corner, usually close to the piano, which we didn't shut away out of sight anymore. It was a part of the room, part of all our lives including Dennis's, and it had had its own role to play within the war's story. Occasionally, I would glimpse Ginger staring at the unoccupied stool, dragging deep on his cigarette, and

I wondered if he wasn't trying to conjure Dennis back to life and, from the hidden recess close by the kitchen door, I willed him with all my being to succeed.

A voice had been silenced too young. A fine generous voice.

Ginger began to invite me to go walking with him. Our promenades were relatively silent. I could say that it was partially due to the language barrier, but that is not really true. Both of us had learned to make ourselves perfectly understood in the other's mother tongue. I believe we both needed the silence yet with the assurance that a friendly soul, an ally, a witness to Dennis's existence, was close to hand. When we spoke it was of Dennis and of England. Ginger vowed that if he survived "this bloody circus", and ever got to see his homeland again, the first thing he would do when he stepped off the train in London would be to visit Dennis's family in Islington and remind them of their son's extraordinary bravery.

"He spoke of them to me," I told him. *Eel and pie*, I grinned to myself. How he missed his eel and pie.

"I know he wrote about you," Ginger replied, resting his hand on my back as we climbed over a stile while crossing two fields speckled with late-autumn flowers – a rare sight in these days of war-torn countryside. "He wanted them to know that he was intending to ask you to marry him."

This crumpled me. For the first time in a long, long

while I allowed my emotions to flow freely in full daylight. I wasn't hidden alone in the cellar, with the shadows and the winey perfume of overripe apples, crying silently, making sure my parents and grandparents could not hear my grief. Ginger jumped down from the stile and stood alongside me. Cautiously, he wrapped his arms about me and I sobbed so loudly into his chest, into the scratchy material of his uniform.

"I don't know how I will live without him," I blubbed.

He squeezed me tighter to him, holding my pain, letting it seep into him, adding it to his own.

"There, there," he muttered.

After that visit, he didn't come back to the Golden Rose. I didn't hear from him even once and I feared that he too had been taken by these hateful hostilities. Like Dennis, had Ginger also been sacrificed to the war?

*

Months went by. Huge armoured machines they are calling "tanks" had appeared in our towns and villages. Like gigantic metal caterpillars, they lumbered through the streets moving no faster than a walking man, sniffing out the countryside, crossing our fields, destroying crops, bullying forward into the heavily shelled landscapes that have become our surrounding reality.

I received no news from Ginger and I began to realize how deeply I valued his friendship. I missed him. I had no one else to talk to about Dennis. No photographs, only my memories and sometimes I grew afraid because the memories would not come. On some days, hard as I tried, I could not picture Dennis in my mind's eye and it felt like a terrible betrayal. I remembered that first evening when Maman asked me to describe him and I had said to her that I had no idea what the pianist looked like and she had sent me back to observe his facial details and report back to her. She had instructed me to take careful note of his every feature so I could remember them.

On the days when I could no longer picture him and the knowledge that he was gone and I would never see him again hit me like a brick, flaying me one more time, I would make myself list his characteristics.

Green eyes.

A grinning countenance.

Blond crinkly hair.

His voice. Such a voice.

Dennis singing with such force and passion…

And whenever I got to "Dennis singing", joy flooded back into my heart. How could I not be happy to have been befriended by such an open, loving generous young man? And he had offered me more than his friendship. I could always cherish in my heart the knowledge that Dennis had loved me and would have made me his wife.

Such a gift had to give me strength. Dennis would want

me to be happy, he would want me to live and to laugh.

Denniz. *Mon* Denniz.

*

Winter was taking hold and the soil was turning to iced clods. Dark, brutal winter. The Battle for the Somme seemed to have moved on elsewhere. A little ground – a matter of a few miles – had been gained but at the cost of millions of lives, including my brother's and Dennis's. How could anybody claim that this was even a small "victory"? Life at *La Rose d'Or* trudged along. What else was there to do? Food was scarce. People were tired. Tired of fighting, of scrabbling to keep going, tired of our fractured identity.

Another year passed and nothing changed. The Americans joined the fray, but we, the population, were losing heart. I was almost nineteen, still a young woman, but encircled by grief and loneliness.

*

And then out of the blue in March of 1918, early one morning, the door of the *auberge* was pushed open. Papa was in the kitchen cooking, preparing the meals for that evening's service. I was tidying and scrubbing the floor.

"Sorry, we are shut," Papa called out.

The dishevelled figure, dirty as a street urchin, paid him no attention. He stumbled on into the room, sullying the newly washed tiles, and fell into a chair. His head cupped into his hands resting on the table, as though he were crying.

Perhaps he was.

"We have no coffee, lad. We've had none for almost two years, and we are closed. Don't expect nourishment here. We've no charity to give," my father called again. He was short-tempered. He frequently was these days, and swung from the range, ready to kick the fellow out. I held him back.

"Wait," I said.

I hurried into the restaurant and rested my arm on the tramp's shoulder.

"It's Hélène," I whispered. I sat down in the chair alongside the man even though the stench coming off him nearly sent me reeling. "Can you hear me? It's Hélène. You are home."

My brother lifted his head from the table and stared hard into my face. He was a shocking sight. His blue eyes shone back at me an electric violet, so vibrant, almost wild were they, in spite of his weariness, against a face blackened by months of living in ditches. His cheeks were hollowed out like a ghost's.

My father was at the kitchen door, as though glued there. "God in heaven," he muttered. "Hélène, get your mother."

I hurried from the café and out into the street, up the courtyard, jumping over the few poultry we still had – the others had been stolen or eaten – calling loudly for Maman. Tears were streaming down my face. I was crying for joy but I was also weeping because I wanted Dennis. I wanted it to be Dennis who had staggered into the bistro, not Pierre.

I feel so ashamed for this thought, this selfish desire. I am overjoyed at the miracle that we have my brother home even though he is very weak and will need constant nursing and Grandma will do the lion's share of that, but in the secret recesses of my heart I found myself asking, "Dear God, why is it that you have allowed Pierre to live, but you have not bestowed the same gift on Dennis?"

Anyone who might have overheard my silent prayer, (none could, of course) would have accused me of arrogance, of pride. I was questioning the will of God. Forgive me.

\*

In spite of my initial reaction, I was very happy to have Pierre home. Slowly, he began to lend Pappy a hand in menial ways, but he refused to go hunting with Papa and Monsieur Balitrand. He said he would never carry a gun again. He never spoke of his experiences during his war years. Perhaps he shared late-night intimate conversations with Papa over glasses of cognac, though I doubt it. With me, he was closed as a clam. Still, without too much difficulty, we began to rebuild our brother and sister relationship. He returned to the land full-time, labouring with our Pappy, who remained a source of strength in spite of his increasing years and the more evident shaking in his hands.

\*

The war ended a month ago. 11th November 1918, after four-and-a-half long years. We, the Allies, are the winning party, if this destroyed landscape seeded with corpses can be judged a victory. France is preparing for Christmas, a muted celebration. For us, it will be our first family Christmas as a complete unit in four years. Pappy is fattening up one of our geese for the occasion. Only yesterday I was thinking that for me there will be one missing at the table. Then, out of the blue, this morning, I received a letter. It was from Ginger. This was the first news I have had from him in almost two years.

He suffered a leg injury in early 1917 and spent several months in a hospital in France recuperating. Having recovered from the bullet, he was sent back to the Front but was gassed in an attack in August of 1917. He was diagnosed medically unfit and traumatized and was sent back to England where he was hospitalized. *"It has been a long haul back to fitness,"* he wrote, *"but now I am steady and ready to join the queues of blokes looking for a job in post-war Britain."*

Once a free man, he paid a visit to Florrie and Walter Stoneham, Dennis's parents in Islington.

*They knew all about me and were over the moon to see me.*

*And they asked after you, Hélène. They would like to meet you. I have suggested to them that when Christmas is over and the weather cheers up a bit, I could accompany them to France. If I have the emotional guts for it, I will take them on a tour and show them where we were billeted and perhaps also to the fields of battle. Importantly, I would like to bring them to the Golden Rose. I know how much it would mean to them. It has been a while now and water has passed beneath our bridges. I have no way of knowing your situation, Hélène, whether Dennis remains in your heart. The truth of the matter is, dear Hélène, I would also like to see you again. You have been in my thoughts frequently, more than frequently, during these days, months and into a year and more of convalescence. Your smile and your beauty have been sources of encouragement to me. If I make the crossing, would you, could you welcome me?*

>*What would you say to such a proposal?*
>*Your loyal, loving friend,*
>*Ginger*

I placed the letter on my small writing desk and walked over to the log fire that warmed my room. I felt the heat of the flames burning into my shins. Across the room through the window, I could see the moon rising, a Christmas moon brightening the flat empty fields on this dark winter's night.

I felt so alone.

*If you were the only girl in the world …* the only girl in the world … his girl…

I could hear Dennis's voice singing to me clearly, even tonight.

Every day. Never a day goes by...

I had missed Ginger. His friendship had been a comfort to me. In our different ways, he and I were both war victims. I would like to see him again and share memories with him. Our thoughts and emotions will always be inspired by one whose voice sung joy into our lives and has been silenced way too young. My Dennis, who loved us both and would wish us both a future, however that might unfold.

*

I returned to my desk and lifted up my pen.

> *Dear Ginger,*
>
> *Even as our Dennis remains in my heart, I will look forward to welcoming you and to meeting Monsieur and Madame Stoneham. I wish you and your family some cheer this Christmas. I will take joy from the fact that a new year is round the corner, a year of peace and friendship.*
>
> *I have also missed you.*
>
> *Hélène*